'Sadie…' Nikos said again, and at long last the finger that rested so lightly on her cheek moved softly.

And he bent his head to kiss her.

It felt as if it was the kiss she had been waiting for all her life. It was shocking, heart-stopping in its gentleness. Sadie's fingers softened, her grip on the water glass loosening so that it fell to the floor. She vaguely heard the splash of water, the thud of the tumbler bouncing on the thick wool of the rug.

But after that she knew nothing else. Nothing ~~but as~~ and the warmth of his body all around ~~her~~ of his arms as they gathered her clo~~se~~ mouth on hers and the magi~~c~~ her lips open, slid his t~~ongue~~ warm softness of her m~~outh~~

She was drowning in a ~~deep sea of~~ sensuality, aware only of the respons~~es that were fl~~owing blindly where Nikos led. Her own ~~lips parted~~, arms winding around his neck, drawing his ~~pr~~oud head down, taking the kiss into another dimension.

'Nikos…' She choked out his name, restless fingers clutching in his hair.

But the words died on her tongue, crushed back down her throat by the way that he suddenly stopped, his whole mood changing. The hands that had held her close were now moving her away from him, setting her aside with cold precision. And then, to her total consternation and horror, he pulled back the cuff of his shirt and checked his watch again.

'Your t~~ime is almost up. You have just fifteen seconds left~~,' he dec~~~~ of emotio~~~~ay before

Kate Walker was born in Nottinghamshire, but as she grew up in Yorkshire she has always felt that her roots are there. She met her husband at university, and originally worked as a children's librarian, but after the birth of her son she returned to her old childhood love of writing. When she's not working, she divides her time between her family, their three cats, and her interests of embroidery, antiques, film and theatre, and, of course, reading. You can visit Kate at www.kate-walker.com

Recent titles by the same author:

KEPT FOR HER BABY
CORDERO'S FORCED BRIDE
BEDDED BY THE GREEK BILLIONAIRE
SPANISH BILLIONAIRE, INNOCENT WIFE
THE GREEK TYCOON'S UNWILLING WIFE

THE KONSTANTOS MARRIAGE DEMAND

BY
KATE WALKER

MILLS & BOON

First published in Great Britain 2009
Paperback edition 2010
Harlequin Mills & Boon Limited,
Eton House, 18-24 Paradise Road, Richmond, Surrey TW9 1SR

© Kate Walker 2009

ISBN: 978 0 263 87767 0

Set in Times Roman 10½ on 12¼ pt
01-0210-54573

Harlequin Mills & Boon policy is to use papers that are natural, renewable and recyclable products and made from wood grown in sustainable forests. The logging and manufacturing process conform to the legal environmental regulations of the country of origin.

Printed and bound in Spain
by Litografia Rosés, S.A., Barcelona

THE KONSTANTOS
MARRIAGE
DEMAND

For Abby Green with thanks
for the inspiration over Kir Royales
in the Shelbourne and for sharing Delphi Lodge

CHAPTER ONE

IN SPITE OF the driving rain that lashed her face, stinging her eyes and almost blinding her, Sadie had no trouble finding her way to the offices where she had an appointment first thing that morning. From the moment that she left the tube station and turned right it was as if her feet were taking her automatically along the route she needed, with no need to look where she was going.

But then of course she had been this way so many times before. In other days, some time ago perhaps, but often enough to know her way without thinking. Of course then she had been heading in this direction in such very different circumstances. In those days she would have arrived in a taxi, or perhaps a chauffeur-driven car, with a uniformed driver sliding the limousine to the edge of the kerb and opening the door for her. Then, the offices towards which she was heading had belonged to her father as the head of Carteret Incorporated. Now they were the UK headquarters of the man who had set out to ruin her family in revenge for the way he had been treated.

And who had succeeded far more than he had ever dreamed.

Burning tears mingled with the sting of the rain as Sadie forced her feet towards the huge plate glass doors that marked the entrance to the elegant building, blinding her so that she almost stumbled across the threshold. Bitter acid swirled in her stomach as the doors slid open and she recognised the way that the words Konstantos Corporation were now etched in big gold letters on the glass where once she had been able to see her father's name—her family name—displayed so clearly.

Would she ever be able to come back here and not think of her father, dead and in his grave for over six months, while the man who had hated him enough to take everything he possessed from him now lorded it over the company that her great-grandfather had built up from nothing into the multi-million corporation it now was?

'No!' Drawing on all the determination she possessed, Sadie shook her head, sending her sleek dark hair flying, her green eyes dark with resolve, as she stepped into the wide, marble-floored foyer. Her black patent high-heeled shoes made a clipped, decisive sound as she made her way across to the pale wood reception desk.

'No!' she muttered under her breath again.

No way was she going to let cruel memories of the past destroy her now. She couldn't let them take away the hard-won strength she had drawn on to get herself here. The resolve that was holding her upright and, she prayed, stopping her legs from shaking, her knees from giving way beneath her. She had come here today because it was her last—her only chance. She had to brave the lion in his den and ask him—beg him— to give them this one small reprieve. Without it the thought of the consequences was impossible to bear. For herself, her mother and her small brother. She couldn't let anything get in the way of that.

'I have an appointment with Mr Konstantos,' she told the smartly dressed young woman behind the reception desk. 'With—Mr Nikos Konstantos.'

She prayed that no tremor in her voice gave away how difficult she had found it to say the name—his name. The name of the man she had once loved almost to the point of madness. The name she had once believed would be hers too for the rest of her life—until she had realised that she was just being used as a pawn in a very nasty power game. A cruel game of revenge and retribution. A settling of scores from wounds that had originally been inflicted long ago and had been many, bitter years festering viciously, until they had poisoned so many lives. Her own amongst them.

'And your name is?' the receptionist enquired.

'Carter,' Sadie supplied, hoping that the sudden dropping of her green eyes to examine some non-existent spot on one of her hands didn't betray how difficult she had found it to come out with the lie. 'S-Sandie Carter.'

She had had to resort to the subterfuge of a false name, she acknowledged inwardly, a nasty taste in her mouth at having been reduced to it. She knew only too well that if she had tried to gain an appointment with him under her real identity then Nikos Konstantos would never even have given her a moment's consideration. Her request to see him would have been refused with cold-blooded arrogance and unyielding rejection. Her attempt to contact him would have been squashed dead under his arrogant heel before it had even struggled into life and she would be back where she had been at the start of this week: lost, desperate, penniless, and without a hope in the world.

She didn't have much of a hope now, but at least the receptionist was checking through a list of names and times on her computer, smiling her satisfaction as she found the fictitious one that Sadie had given her, and making a swift click with her mouse as she checked it off.

'You're a little early…'

'Not to worry—I can wait…' Sadie put in hastily, knowing

only too well that 'a little early' was a major understatement. She was way too early—by more than half an hour. But nervousness and a real fear that she might have backed out of this if she hadn't left home just as soon as she was ready had pushed her out of the door well before the time needed for her journey.

'No need,' the other woman assured her. 'Mr Konstantos's first appointment cancelled, so he can see you straight away.'

'Thank you,' Sadie managed, because it was all she could say.

She'd committed herself to this interview and she had to go through with it. But now that the time had come she felt sick at just the thought of confronting Nikos here, in what had once been her family's offices. What had possessed her to do this? To think that she could cope with seeing Nikos for the first time in five years, and come back into the building that did so much to emphasise how far her family's fortunes had fallen—both at the same time.

'I think perhaps…' she began again, her already shaky courage deserting her, meaning to say that she'd changed her mind—she had another appointment, or her mother had just called…anything to give her an excuse to leave, get out of here now. To run and hide before she had to come face to face with…

'Mr Konstantos…'

The receptionist's tone, her sudden change of expression, would have alerted Sadie to just what was happening even without the use of that emotive name. The other woman's eyes had widened, her gaze going straight to a point over Sadie's shoulder, behind her back. And the expression in it, as in the way she had said the name—*that name*—told Sadie without another word needing to be spoken just who had come up behind her, silent as a hunting jungle cat, and possibly just as deadly.

'Has my ten-o'clock appointment arrived?'

'She's right here…'

The receptionist smiled as she indicated Sadie standing before her desk, and she clearly thought that Sadie would smile back. Smile and turn. Possibly say hello or some such.

But Sadie knew that she couldn't move. Her legs seemed to have frozen to the spot. Her mind too had iced up, leaving her incapable of registering a single thought other than the fact that he was behind her.

That *Nikos Konstantos* was right behind her. And that at any moment he would see her and realise who she was.

It was the voice that had done it. Just those few words in those deep, sensually husky tones had short-circuited her brain waves, making it impossible to think of anything but the shivering sensations that ran up and down her spine. Once she had heard that voice whisper to her in the darkness, murmuring sounds of delight and promising her the very best—the world—the future. And, entranced by that sexy accent, lost in the world of sensuality that just being with him had always created around her, she had foolishly, naively believed in every word.

Every lying word.

'Mrs Carter?'

Her silence had gone on too long. It had had the opposite effect to the one she had hoped for. What she had really wanted was to become invisible. Or for the beautiful marble floor to open up so that she could fall right through, out of sight. But instead, by standing still and silent, she had puzzled and confused the other woman so that she frowned in faint enquiry, making a slight nod of her head to draw Sadie's attention to the man behind her.

A man who couldn't possibly be unaware of the way she was standing there, stiff and awkward and with blatant disregard for normal polite behaviour.

'This is Mrs Carter...' The receptionist tried again. 'Your ten o'clock...'

She had to move; she had no choice. Any more delay and she would raise all his suspicions, put him on edge. Drawing on all her strength and squaring her shoulders, Sadie snatched in a deep, sharp breath and turned on her heel. The effort she put into the movement made it far too strong, too wild, so that she whirled round, almost spinning out of control as she came suddenly face to face with the man she had once believed she was destined to marry.

He recognised her instantly, of course. No matter how much she might have changed over the past five years—and she had changed—she knew that. She had to have changed. There was no way she could still be the younger, more re-laxed, far happier Sadie who had first met Nikos. But there was no doubt, no hesitation in his recognition of her. She saw the way that his face changed, the sudden tightening of his mouth, the flare of something wild and dangerous in his eyes, and her blood ran cold inside her veins at the sight.

'You!' he said, and that was all. The one word was riddled with all the disgust, contempt and obvious hatred that he felt for her, making her shiver inwardly in fearful response.

'Me,' she managed, sheer nerves making her tone inappropriately flippant, so that she saw the way that anger snapped his dark straight brows together in an ominous glare. 'Hello, Nikos.'

'My office—*now*,' he said, and spun on his heel, striding away across the foyer, never once looking back, and obviously believing that she would follow. That she would have no option but to obey the harshly muttered command he had flung at her.

And really, she did have no option. It was either that or leave, with her mission unaccomplished. And now that she had braved the lion in his den, surely she had the worst over with?

Or did she? It was true that she'd been pushed into this meeting she'd been dreading, but she had had no time to prepare, or even to think about what she was going to say. And she had hoped to approach Nikos as calmly and quietly as possible. Instead she had done just the opposite.

She'd knocked him off balance too, and he was angry as a result. Coldly furious.

It was there in every inch of his long, powerful body as he strode across the foyer towards the lifts. It stiffened the straight spine, tightened the powerful shoulders and held his dark head so arrogantly high that she felt it gave him an even more impressive height than usual.

It was impossible not to reflect on the sheer impact of that stunning frame, the width of chest, narrow sexy hips and long, long legs. She had rarely seen him quite so formally dressed when she had known him before, and the effect of the severely tailored outfit was to turn him into a distant, unapproachable figure. Deep inside there was an ache in her heart at the memory of the younger, warmer, kinder Nikos.

At least he had seemed warmer and kinder then. It was only later that she had discovered the truth about how he really was.

'Are you coming?'

The sharp question dragged her back to the present with a jolt. *Warm* and *kind* were not the words to use about Nikos now. In fact, in everything about him he was the exact opposite. As he stood just inside the lift, one long finger jammed hard on the button that held the door open, he directed a cold, icy glare at her face that had her jumping into action fast, almost scurrying the last few steps into the compartment and huddling back against the wall.

Nikos's only response was a sharp movement that released the button, letting the door slide to, shutting them in.

'I…' Sadie tried, but another of those arctic glares froze the words on her tongue.

She had forgotten how deep a bronze his eyes could be in

certain lights. In others they could be almost molten gold, the colour of the purest honey and just as sweet—or they had been once upon a time. There was nothing sweet in the look he turned on her now, nothing to melt the knot of ice that seemed to have clenched around her stomach, twisting it brutally until she felt raw and nauseous deep inside.

And Nikos clearly had no intention of even attempting to lighten the atmosphere or to make her feel any better. Instead he simply leaned back against the wall of the compartment, folding his strong arms across the width of his chest as he subjected her to the sort of savage scrutiny that made her feel as if the burn of his gaze might actually shrivel her where she stood. Why she didn't just collapse into a pile of ashes under it she didn't know. Instead, she shifted awkwardly from one foot to another then, unable to bear the terrible silence any longer, forced herself to try again.

'I—I can explain…' was all she managed, before he made a slicing, brutal gesture with his hand that cut off all attempt at speech.

'In my office.'

It was tossed at her, almost flung into her face, no hint of expression or trace of warmth on his features. His expression was a stone wall, no light in his eyes, his jaw set and hard.

'But I…' she tried again.

'In my office,' he repeated, and his tone left her in no doubt that he would brook no argument so there was no use in even trying.

Besides, the confined space of the lift was too small, too claustrophobic for her to want to risk confronting him while she was trapped there. She might have been prepared to face him in his office—in more civilised surroundings—but not here, not now. Not like this.

And, seeing the burn of icy anger in those golden eyes, she

felt a shiver creep across her skin at the thought that *civilised* no longer seemed an appropriate word to describe Nikos Konstantos, either.

'In your office, then,' she muttered, determined not to let him have the last word, and the glance she turned in his direction had the flash of defiance in its green depths.

That glance challenged him to take things further, Nikos acknowledged grimly as he adjusted his broad shoulders against the mirrored wall of the lift. But if she knew just what sort of taking it further was actually in his thoughts then he suspected that she would back down pretty hastily. Back down and back away.

It was what he should do too. The back away part at least. He should back away, back off, get his thoughts under control. He had been rocked, knocked mentally off balance by the speed and intensity of his response to discovering that she was in the building. That his ten-o'clock appointment was actually with none other than Sadie Carteret.

With the woman who had once taken him for a fool, used him, fleeced him, damn nearly been the death of his father, and then walked out on him on what had been supposed to be their wedding day. Bile rose in his throat at just the thought. The memory should have been enough to blast his mind with black hatred, drive any more basic, more masculine response right out of it.

But instead it was desire that had hit. No—give it its proper name—it had been lust. Pure, driven, primitive male lust. Though of course there had been nothing at all pure about the thoughts that had sizzled through his mind. And that had been from only seeing her from the back.

He had taken one look at the tall, slender frame of the woman in front of him, gaze lingering on the swell of her hips, the pert bottom under the clinging navy blue skirt. The contrast between the very feminine curves and the surprisingly matronly clothing, the soft flesh pushing against the restricting material, had had a sensual kick that had made his head spin and he had known that he was resolved to get to know this Sandie Carter well—very well—as swiftly as possible.

But then she had turned and he had seen that she was not Sandie Carter at all but Sadie Carteret, the woman who had torn his world apart five years before and was now, it seemed, back in his life.

For what?

'I suppose things will be more private there,' she added now, smoothing a hand over her hair and then, more revealingly, down the sides of her hips, as if wiping away some nervous perspiration from her palms and fingers.

She was not as much in control as she wanted to appear and that suited him fine. He wanted her off balance, on edge with her guard down. That way she might let slip the truth about what she was after. Because she was after something—she had to be.

'And you'd prefer to continue this interview in private?'

'Wouldn't you?'

It was another challenge, one that brought her head up, green eyes flashing, her neat chin lifting high.

'That is why you want to continue things in your office, isn't it?'

'I prefer not to have the whole world knowing my business.'

He'd had enough of that when she'd swept into his life like a whirlwind and stormed out again, leaving everything turned upside down and inside out. It had been bad enough that the financial newspapers had delighted in reporting the downfall of the Konstantos business empire with barely disguised glee, but the memory of his personal humiliation at the hands of the gossip columns and the paparazzi made acid burn in his stomach as the bitter taste of hatred filled his mouth.

'Me too.'

Something in his words or his tone had hit home, making her change her stance and drop her eyes suddenly, looking down at the floor.

So did she have something to hide? Something she would prefer the papers never got their hands on? Something he could use to bring her down as low as she had brought him? A rich sense of satisfaction ran darkly through his blood at the thought.

'Then in this at least we are in agreement.'

And he would have to control his need to know more, to understand just why she was here. To stamp down on the sudden rush of anticipation that was almost like an electrical charge along his senses. A call to battle and a challenge to be met. Once they were inside his office things would be different. Then he would get the truth from her.

Although the fact was that he already largely suspected he knew what that truth would be. Deep down he knew just why she was here because there really could only be one answer to that question.

She had to be here for money.

What else would bring her here, knocking at his door? That was what she would have most need of after all. When he'd brought her father down, he'd destroyed her luxurious way of life too. And now that Edwin Carteret was dead, there was no one else she could turn to.

But she must be desperate to think of asking him for help. Just how desperate she'd shown by lying about her name. She'd known that there was no way that Sadie Carteret would ever have been allowed to set foot over the threshold.

So why was he taking her up to his office instead of having Security eject her—forcibly, if needed—from the building?

He wasn't prepared to admit even to himself that the decision had anything to do with the instant physical response he'd felt in the first moments when he'd seen her. And now, in this small compartment, with the tall, slender lines of her body, the sleek, shining mane of dark hair and the porcelain smooth pallor of her skin repeated over and over in the multitude of reflections in the walled mirrors, it was so much worse to handle. The scent of her skin came to him on a waft of air with each movement she made, and when she shook back that smooth bell of hair it was mixed with a soft, herbal essence that made his head and his thoughts spin. Primitive hunger clawed at him deep inside, and the clutch of desire that twisted low down made him shift uncomfortably, needing to ease the discomfort.

Thankfully at that moment the lift came to a halt and the heavy metal doors slid open on to the grey carpeted corridor that led to his office. Deliberately Nikos stood back and gestured to indicate that Sadie should precede him, refusing to allow himself to look anywhere but at the top of her shining dark-haired head as she moved past.

'Left,' he said sharply, then swallowed down the rest of the directions as to how to reach his office. Because of course she didn't need them. She knew the way to what had once been her father's office probably better than he did, and she was already heading in that direction without any help from him.

She'd made a *faux pas* there, Sadie admitted to herself. She'd probably infuriated him by not standing back and waiting for directions but setting out at once in the right direction. But she'd just turned to the left automatically, following her path from so many other times in the past. She could only be grateful for the fact that walking ahead of Nikos gave her a moment or two to adjust her expression unseen, to control the sudden waver in her composure, the instinctive tightening of her mouth at the faint shiver that ran down her spine.

She had to remember that she no longer belonged here. That she wasn't on her home territory but in Nikos's domain. This was where he belonged now, where he ruled like some king of ancient Greece, absolute monarch of all he surveyed.

Absolute monarch—and possibly a tyrant too? She didn't know what Nikos was like as a boss, but he had to be a ruthless and highly efficient one. It had only taken him five short years to turn round the fortunes of the Konstantos Corporation from the weakened position in which his father's wild gambling on the stock exchange had left it. He'd turned the tables on *her* father, exacting a brutal revenge for the way Edwin had treated him in the past.

'I'm sorry…'

Carefully she adjusted her pace so that she was no longer leading but had made space for Nikos to walk alongside her, take the lead if he preferred. But he didn't take advantage of the change. Instead he stayed just behind her, a dark, looming shape at her right shoulder. Impossible to see. Impossible to judge his mood.

He was so close that she could almost feel the heat of his body reaching out to her. The scent of some cool, crisp after-shave tantalised her nostrils with thoughts of the ozone tang of the clear blue sea off the shores of the private island that the Konstantos family had once owned. That island had been part of the property empire Edwin had taken from them, so she supposed that it must now be once more back in Nikos's hands—unless her father had sold it on to someone else.

Her conscience gave an uncomfortable little twist at the thought, knowing how much Nikos had loved that island. It had meant as much to him as Thorn Trees, the old house that had been part of her family for so long, meant to her mother. So surely he would understand why she had come here today.

'Here…'

The touch of Nikos's hand on her arm to bring her to a halt outside a door was soft and swift, barely there and then gone again, but all the same the faint brush of his fingers against her elbow sizzled right the way through to her skin underneath the fine navy wool, making her almost stumble in reaction. She had known that touch in the past, had felt it so intimately on her body, on her hungry flesh without any barrier of clothes. She'd felt his touch, his caress, his kiss along every yearning inch of her, and now, like a violin fine-tuned to a maestro's hand, she felt herself quiver deep inside in shivering response as much to her memories as to the heat of his hand that barely reached her in reality.

'I know!'

Unease pushed the words from her, as she faked impatience and irritation as an excuse to snatch her arm away from his hand as she twisted the door handle with unnecessary force and wrenched it open.

'Of course you do.' Nikos's response was darkly cynical, the rough edge to his voice a warning that she had overstepped the mark as he reached a long arm across her shoulder and pushed at the door. 'But allow me...'

Could the words be any more pointed? Could he make it any plainer that he was emphasising the fact that *he* owned this place now? That he, and not she, was in the position of power. Very definitely in charge.

And she would do well to remember that, Sadie told herself, pulling her scurrying thoughts back under control, forcing herself to take a couple of deep, calming breaths and remind herself just why she was here. She needed Nikos on her side and she would be foolish to anger and alienate him before she had even had a chance to put her case.

'Thank you.'

Somehow she managed to make it polite, careful. Not quite

the polite, submissive murmur she suspected would be more politic, but politic was beyond her. Her heart was pounding, ragged and uneven, so that her breath was jerky and raw. Tension, she told herself. Pure, unadulterated tension. She was nervous about what was coming, fearful about what she had to say and the way he might receive it.

It couldn't be anything else, she told herself. It had to be that, could only be that. She wasn't going to let it be anything else that was affecting her in this way. But with the heady scent of clean male skin in her nostrils, the brush of his hand along her neck as he reached for the door, the memory of those long ago sensual touches and caresses coming so very close to the surface of her mind, she knew that something else was knocking her dangerously off balance. Something she didn't want to look at too closely for fear of what she might find.

'Come in.'

Nikos was still keeping to that excessively polite tone, the one that warned her that she was in the presence of real danger. That she was trapped with a dark and menacing predator, one that had simply been biding its time before it decided to turn and pounce. And once inside this office, in the privacy that he had declared he was determined on, with no one close at hand to hear or to intervene should she need them, that surely would be the moment that he finally resolved to attack.

That thought made her legs suddenly weak as cotton wool beneath her as she stumbled into the room, coming halfway across the office before they gave up completely and brought her to nervous halt, not knowing what to do next. And as she stood there, her thoughts whirling, trying to find some way of beginning, an opening that would start her off on the path to saying what she had come to say, the words to ask for what she needed so badly, she felt Nikos brush past her. He strode towards the big desk that dominated the room, his movements brusque and controlled, his long body held taut with some ruthlessly restrained emotion. And it was as he swung round to face her that she saw the dark expression etched onto his stunning features and felt her heart lurch painfully just once, before it plummeted downwards to somewhere beneath the soles of her neat patent court shoes.

Anger. The whole set of his face was tight with icy fury, his golden eyes blazing with it. Away from public scrutiny, from everyone else who might see them together, hear what he had to say, he had thrown off the careful veneer of civilised, cultured politeness. The real Nikos—dark, primitive and very, very angry—was exposed in total clarity, without any pretence to mute the shocking impact of the rage that gripped him. A rage that was directed straight at her.

The predator had decided to pounce—and this time he was very definitely going in for the kill.

CHAPTER TWO

'You LIED!' NIKOS said, flinging the accusation at her almost as soon as the door had swung closed behind her, shutting them in together. 'You lied about who you were—gave a false name.'

'Of course I did!'

Sadie prayed that the control she was forcing into her voice kept it steady. She hoped that she had at least held it down so that it didn't go soaring up too high under the influence of the panic that was tying her insides into tight, painful knots.

'I had to. What else could I do? If I'd given my real name then there's no way you would have ever agreed to see me, would you?'

'You're damn right I wouldn't. You wouldn't have got across the threshold. But the fact remains that you are here—and that you lied in order to get here. Which means that you have something you want to say. Something that is important enough for you to use that lie in order to get to say it. So what is that, I wonder?'

The look he turned on her seemed to sear right through her, the blaze of his eyes so intense that Sadie almost expected to see her clothes scorch and burn along the path that it traced over her body.

Nikos was behind his desk, and he leaned forward to stab

one long finger down on a button by his phone. Sadie heard a woman's voice, faintly blurred by the nervous buzzing in her head, respond almost immediately.

'No calls.' It was a command, and clearly one he meant to have obeyed. 'And no interruptions. I am not to be disturbed until I say.'

And if the secretary or PA goes against those instruction, then she's a braver woman than I am, Sadie told herself. But the next moment any other thoughts fled from her mind as Nikos nodded his satisfaction and turned his attention back to her.

'So why are you here?'

'I…'

Faced with that arctic glare, the ferocious bite of his demand, Sadie found that in that moment she couldn't actually recall precisely why she *was* there, let alone form her response into any sort of coherent argument. One that might actually impress him, persuade him on to her side when she knew that he was guaranteed to take the opposite stance, simply because he was who he was and she was the one doing the asking.

She was suddenly very glad of the expanse of polished wood of his desk that came between them, acting as a barrier between the powerful dynamic force that was Nikos Konstantos.

It was totally irrational, but when he glowered at her like that she suddenly felt as if the room had shrunk, as if the walls had moved inwards, the ceiling coming down, contracting the space around her until she felt it hard to breathe. She felt trapped, confined in a room that had suddenly become too small to hold them both.

She had been shut in with him in the lift, in a far smaller space, but somehow, contradictorily, this seemed so much worse. Now Nikos seemed so much bigger, so much more powerful, dominating the space in which he stood and holding her captive simply by the pure force of his presence.

Or was it about the room? Because it was the office that had once been her father's? But there was no sign at all of the previous occupant. Every last trace of anything that was personal to Edwin had been removed and replaced with something much more modern, more stylish—and much more expensive. Even in the good days of Carteret Incorporated the office had never looked like this.

The heavy, dark desk and chairs had all been removed and replaced by modern furniture in a pale wood. Thick golden rugs covered the floor, and in the window area there was a comfortable-looking settee and armchairs for relaxing.

It spoke of Nikos Konstantos of Konstantos Corporation. The man who had taken everything her father had thrown at him and refused to go down under it. He had seen everything his own father had worked for snatched away, had stared bankruptcy and total ruin in the face and still come out fighting. And in five short years he had built up his business empire to what it had once been—and then outstripped that. The Konstantos Corporation was bigger, stronger, richer than it had ever been. And it had swallowed up Carteret Incorporated and absorbed it whole on its way to the top.

And Nikos *was* the Konstantos Corporation.

As she hesitated, Nikos shot back the cuff on his immaculate white shirt and glanced swiftly and pointedly at his watch.

'You have five minutes to explain yourself—and that is more than you would have had if I'd known it was you,' he stated curtly. 'Five minutes. No more.'

Which was guaranteed to dry Sadie's tongue, make it feel as if it was sticking to the roof of her mouth, and no matter how hard she swallowed, she couldn't quite force herself to speak.

'Could—could we sit down?' she tried, looking longingly

at the cream cushions on the padded chairs. Perhaps with her attention taken off the need to concentrate on keeping her legs from shaking so that she could stay upright she might manage to put her thoughts—and the necessary arguments to convince him—into some sort of coherent order.

Sitting down was the last thing Nikos had in mind. He had no intention of letting her get settled, allowing her to stay a moment longer than he had to. Just seeing her here like this was making him feel as if the room was suddenly at the centre of a wild and dangerous hurricane, with the day he had been living being picked up and whirled around, turned inside out.

And the sound of her voice was raking up memories he had pushed to the back of his mind for so long. He wanted them to stay there. He had never wanted to speak to Sadie Carteret ever again.

'Tell him to go away, Daddy.'

The words she had tossed down the staircase at him, the last words he had ever heard her speak on the day that had been the worst day of his life, came back to haunt him, making savage anger flare like rocket fire inside his head.

'Tell him the only interest he had for me was his money, and now that he has none I never want to see him again.'

And he had never wanted to see her, Nikos acknowledged, his whole body taut with rejection of her presence in his life once more. The disturbing tug of sensuality he had felt in the lift had evaporated, he was thankful to find. The memory of her callous rejection, the cold tight voice in which she'd flung it at him, not even bothering to come downstairs and tell him face to face, had driven that away, leaving behind just a cold savagery of hatred.

The sooner she said what she had to say and got out of here, the better.

'Five minutes,' he repeated with deadly emphasis. 'And

then I get Security to escort you out. You've wasted one of them already.'

'I wanted to talk to you about buying Thorn Trees!'

That got his attention. His dark head went back, eyes narrowing sharply.

'Buying? What is this? Have you suddenly come into a fortune?'

Belatedly Sadie realised her mistake. Nerves had got the better of her and she'd blurted out the first thing that came into her mind.

'No—of course not.'

'I didn't mean buy—I could never afford that. I just…'

The sudden drop of those bronze eyes down to the gold watch on his wrist, watching the second hand tick by, incensed her, pushing her into rash, unguarded speech.

'Damn you, you took everything we had. Every last thing my father had owned—except for this. I just hoped that I might be able to rent it from you.'

'Rent?'

Her antagonism had been a mistake, sparking off an answering anger in Nikos, one that tightened every muscle in his face, thinning his lips to a hard, tight line.

'That house is a handsome property in a prime position in London. With some restoration—a lot of restoration, admittedly—it would sell for a couple of million—maybe more. Why should I want to rent it out to you?'

'Because I need it.'

Because my mother's happiness—possibly even her sanity—her life—might depend on it. But Sadie wasn't quite ready to expose every last detail of the worries that had driven her to come here today to plead with him. Not with Nikos standing there, dark and imposing, arms now folded across the width of his chest, jaw clamped tight, eyes as cold as golden ice, looking for all the world like the judge in some criminal court. And one who was just about to put the black cap on his head, ready to pronounce the sentence of execution.

Besides, her mother had already lost so very much. She wouldn't deprive her of the last shreds of her dignity, her privacy, unless she really had no choice.

'As you've admitted, it needs a great deal of restoration. There's no way you would be able to get the market value for it right now.'

'And no way I can get the necessary renovations done with you and your mother there. I thought I'd given instructions to my solicitor…'

'You did.'

Oh, he had. She knew that only too well. The letter advising her family that Nikos Konstantos now owned Thorn Trees and that they should vacate the house by the end of the month had arrived a few days before. It had only been by a stroke of luck that Sadie had managed to intercept the envelope before her mother had shown any interest in the post. That way she had succeeded in keeping the bad news from Sarah for a while at least.

But not for good. Within twenty-four hours, her mother had somehow found the envelope and read its contents. Her panicked reaction had been everything Sadie had anticipated—and most dreaded. It was the final straw that had pushed her into action, bringing her to the realisation that there was only one way she could hope to handle this and that that was by going to see Nikos himself, appealing directly to his better nature in the hope that he would help them, let them stay at least until things improved just a little.

Not that Nikos, as he was now, looked as if he had a better nature at all. His face was set and stony, his eyes like glowing flints.

'Your solicitor did exactly as you told him—don't worry about that.'

'Then you know what I have planned for the house. And it does not include a couple of sitting tenants.'

'But we don't have anywhere to go.'

'Find somewhere.'

Could his voice get any more brutal, any more unyielding? There wasn't even a flicker of emotion in it, nothing she could hope to appeal to. And what made it so much worse was the way a memory danced in front of her eyes. An image of the same man but five years younger. And so unlike the cold-faced monster who seemed intent on glaring her into submission that he looked like someone else entirely.

She'd loved that other man. Loved him so much she'd broken her own heart rather than break his. Only to find that in the end he hadn't had a heart to break.

A terrible sense of loss stabbed at her and she felt bitter tears burn at the back of her eyes. She only managed to hold them back by sheer force of will.

'It isn't as easy as that,' she managed, her voice rough and uneven. 'In case you hadn't noticed, the economy…'

She swallowed down the last of the sentence, knowing that finishing it would only give him more ammunition to use against her. Of course he knew all about the economy, and the way things had changed so dramatically in a couple of years or so. It was what he had used against Edwin, manipulating the wild fluctuations in the stock market to his personal advantage and against the man he had hated so bitterly.

'I thought that you had a business of your own,' Nikos said now.

'A small one.'

And one that wasn't doing very well at all, Sadie acknowledged privately. With things as tight as they were for most people, no one was indulging in the luxury of having a wedding planner organise their 'big day'. She hadn't had an enquiry in weeks—and as for bookings, well, the last she'd had had cancelled the next month.

'Then get yourself another house. There are plenty on the market.'

'I can't afford—'

'Can't afford a smaller house but yet you want me to rent you Thorn Trees? Have you thought about this? About the sort of rent that can be asked for a place like that?'

'Yes, I've thought about it.'

And had quailed inside at the realisation of the fact that just the rent on her family home would probably be far more than she could possibly manage to rake together every month.

'Or did you perhaps think that I might be a soft touch and give it to you for—what is that you say—mate's rates?'

The slang term sounded weird on his tongue, his accent suddenly seeming so much thicker than before, mangling the words until they were almost incomprehensible. But even more disturbing was the knowledge that there was no way at all that they applied to the relationship between herself and Nikos. Whatever else they had been, they had never been 'mates'. Never truly friends or anything like it. Hot, passionate lovers, fiancés, prospective bride and groom—or at least that was what had been intended.

Or had it? She had been overjoyed to accept Nikos's proposal. Had looked forward to her wedding day with joyful anticipation and had wept out her devastated heart when she had been forced to cancel it. But what she had thought had been a broken heart had been as nothing when compared to the misery she had endured later, when she had learned the truth about what Nikos had really been planning.

The shattering of her dreams had coincided with such a

major crisis in her family life that she had barely known what she was doing from day to day. In the end she had resorted to the policy of least resistance, letting her father dictate everything she did, the way she behaved. He had written the script for those appalling days and she had followed it exactly. At least that way her mother had been safe, and Edwin Carteret had made sure that Nikos had failed in his attempts to get back into her life, to try and see Sadie—and no doubt hurt her even more.

'I…'

'Get yourself another house, Sadie,' Nikos commanded. 'Nothing else is on offer.'

'I don't want another house—I want…'

I want Thorn Trees was all she had to say. And then he would ask her *why*.

And if she answered with the truth, how would he react? Would he sympathise, as the Nikos she'd thought she had known all those years ago would have sympathised? Or would the Nikos he was now see yet another opportunity to further deepen his revenge against the family who had ruined his father and taken almost everything from him?

Not knowing whether telling him the truth would help or simply put another weapon into his hands, she swallowed hard against the uncomfortable dryness of her throat.

'Look…'

Her voice croaked embarrassingly.

'Do you think I could have a coffee or something? Even some water?'

Seeing the look he gave her, she felt her heart clench at the savage contempt that burned in his eyes.

'Of course not,' she commented bitterly. 'That would eat into the paltry five minutes you've allotted me. It's all right.'

Despair blurred her eyes, tiredness making the room seem

to swing round her. Why didn't she just admit defeat, give up and go home? But the memory of her mother's face as she'd left the house was there, urging her to try again. Sarah needed a home and so did little George. And right now Sadie was their only chance of keeping the house.

'Here…'

The abrupt word made her start, jump back slightly. Nikos sounded suddenly so very close. Disturbingly so. She blinked hard to clear her vision and found herself staring at a glass filled with water, bubbles rising inside, beads of moisture sliding down the sides. Feeling as she did, it had the effect of discovering a cool oasis in the centre of a blazing desert.

'Thank you.' It was genuinely grateful.

Reaching out a hand to take the glass from him, she misjudged the distance, the right approach, and found that although she aimed to grasp it at the base, well below his hand, in fact she closed her fingers over his, feeling their strong warmth in contrast to the cold hardness of the glass.

'I'm sorry!'

A sensation like the shock from a bolt of lightning shot up all the nerves in her arm, so that she wanted to snatch her hand away, and yet at the same time it seemed that the sudden heat had welded their fingers together, so she couldn't peel hers away without a terrible effort.

Nikos seemed to have no such problem, though his eyes held hers, darkly mesmeric, as he adjusted his hold on the glass, eased his hand away, waiting just a moment to make sure that she had a good grip before he finally let his arm drop to his side.

Still with their eyes locked together, Sadie lifted the glass of water to her parched lips, swallowed a mouthful, finding it suddenly intensely difficult to force the cool liquid past the disturbing knot that seemed to have closed off her throat.

She wished he would look away, and yet at the same time she knew that she would feel lost and strangely bereft if he did.

'Thank…'

Her voice failed her, seeming to shrivel in the heat of that intent gaze. Something had happened to his eyes, so that the colour of the iris seemed to have disappeared and there were just the deep dark pools of his widened pupils, edged only at the rim with burning molten bronze.

Almost snatching at the glass, she drank again, gulping down water that did nothing to cool the sudden heat that had flooded her body or ease the sudden heavy pounding of her heart.

'Thank you.'

At least her voice sounded stronger now, without that appalling crack in the middle that gave away far too much of what she was feeling.

She held out the glass to him, expecting him to take it back, check his watch again to see just how long of her allotted time she had left. But instead, to her total shock, he ignored the gesture and, extending one long, tanned finger, reached out to touch it to her cheek just below the corner of her right eye. Instinctively Sadie flinched and would have backed away, but once more something in that intent expression caught and held her frozen where she was.

'Tears?' he said on a softly spoken note of blank disbelief. 'Tears—for a *house!*'

Tears?

Sadie's hand flew up to her face, the backs of her fingers brushing her cheek to discover the shocking truth of his words. Tears that she had been totally unaware of having shed had slipped onto her skin, moistening her eyelashes. But even as she recognised that they were there, she looked deep into Nikos's darkly assessing gaze and knew a terrible sense of despair as she acknowledged that he couldn't be more wrong about the reason why they were there.

'Not just a house.'

Had she said the words aloud or just heard them inside her head? She couldn't tell, only knew that they blazed so hard they seemed to be etched into her thoughts in letters of fire.

Not just the house—not even though it was the home that she loved, that her mother needed. It wasn't anything to do with Thorn Trees or even her angry frustration at not being able to persuade Nikos round to her way of thinking that was twisting a brutal knife in her devastated heart. Instead it was the sudden terrible sense of loss that she'd known in the moment she'd looked into Nikos's eyes as he came close to her.

She'd armoured herself against this meeting. Told herself that what she had once felt for him was all over, that time had healed the scars and put a distance between her and the love she had once felt for this man. That his final betrayal and the way he had behaved since, the terrible revenge he had exacted so cold-bloodedly, had left her immune to him, not even hatred surviving of the onslaught of feelings she had been through.

But if this was immunity, then she would hate to have to try and face a fully developed fever! Her whole body was fizzing with awareness, coming to burning life in response to just that one, tiny touch.

No—not just the touch. She was responding to the look in his darkened eyes, the scent of his skin, the sound of his voice, even of his soft breathing, his very presence. Everything about him made her burn as if she stood in the direct line of the sun. And yet, contradictorily, it held her frozen to the spot, unable to move or look away. And hunger, dark and disturbing physical craving, throbbed like a heavy pulse in her blood.

'It's not just a house,' she tried again, hoping to stir him into movement, away from her.

But it seemed that Nikos too had fallen under something of the same spell. After that one harsh question he stood as transfixed as her. His eyes locked with hers, his burning gaze so fixed, so unwavering that it seemed he barely even blinked. And Sadie sensed rather than actually saw the way his long tanned throat moved as he swallowed deeply.

'Sadie…' he said at last, his voice seeming to be becoming unravelled at the edges.

And the sound of her name on his lips had the effect of stabbing a stiletto dagger right into the centre of her heart, so that it jolted once, violently, then started pattering rapidly, high up in her throat, making it so very difficult to breathe naturally. His accent had deepened shockingly on the sound, making it raw and rough, disturbingly like the times that she heard him speak her name in the burn of passion, deep in the darkness of the night.

Memory dried her mouth again and nervously she licked her lips to ease the sensation. The water seemed to have done nothing at all to ease her thirst, or if it had then the moisture had evaporated in the heat that his touch had sent rushing through her.

'Sadie…' Nikos said again, and at long last the finger that rested so lightly on her cheek moved softly.

But not to move away from her, not to break the contact with her skin. Instead, his touch simply shifted, adjusted slightly, smoothing down one side of her cheek to curl under the fine line of her jaw, lifting her chin. She heard his harshly indrawn breath, watched those heavy black eyelashes close slowly, then open again as the burning bronze of his gaze blazed into her.

And he bent his head to kiss her.

It felt as if she had been waiting for it for so long. As if it was the kiss she had been waiting for all her life. It was shocking, heart-stopping in its gentleness. In anyone else she might even have called it hesitancy, but there was nothing hesitant about Nikos's taking of her mouth. It was slow, it was sensual, it was totally sure of what he was doing—the effect it was aiming for. It was pure seduction, aimed right at her libido and having exactly the effect that he wanted.

Sadie's fingers softened, her grip on the water glass loosening so that it fell to the floor. She vaguely heard the splash of water, the thud of the tumbler bouncing on the thick wool of the rug.

But after that she knew nothing else. Nothing but Nikos and the warmth of his body all around her. The strength of his arms as they gathered her close. The pressure of his mouth on hers and the magic it was working as he eased her lips open, slid his tongue along the edge and into the warm softness of her mouth.

His hands slid up her back, into her hair, tangling in the dark silky strands. He twisted his fingers around them, using them to hold her head just where he wanted as he increased the pressure, forcing her to open to him even more.

She was drowning in a dark, heady world of sensuality. Lost to reality and aware only of the responses of her body, following blindly where Nikos led. She was soft and malleable in his hands, unable to think for herself or find any trace of will to call her own. Her own hands lifted, arms winding themselves around his neck, drawing his proud head down even closer, taking the kiss into another dimension, another stage of hungry sensuality.

'Nikos…' she murmured against his cheek as he turned his head, his wicked, beguiling mouth finding the fine, taut line of her throat and kissing his way down it to the spot where her pulse throbbed frantically at the base of her neck.

When his warm lips pressed against the tiny point, she felt

her breath catch in her throat, the electric shocks of response sparking its way along every nerve, flashing down to pool in liquid heat in the most intimate spot low in her body, between her legs. Restlessly, she moved against him, pressing her body close to the hardness of his and feeling the heated swelling of the erection that marked his undisguised response to her. That pressure was what she wanted. That and more—so much more—and it was obvious that Nikos felt the same as one large hard hand came down to curve over her buttocks, bringing her into even more intimate contact and holding her there.

'Nikos…' Once more she choked out his name, restless fingers clutching in his hair, pressing against his scalp, holding him against her.

It seemed that the heat of their bodies had melted her bones, so that she swayed against him on unsteady legs. She heard his breath hiss in sharply between his teeth, and the hand that had been in her hair released her to slide, hot and sensuous, down to her ribcage to cup the side of her breast, his thumb stroking tormentingly over her nipple, bringing it to springing, tightened life underneath the cotton of her blouse. Sadie's own breath caught in her throat, making her gasp in shocked delight and wriggle even closer, pressing her sensitised flesh against the heat of his palm.

'Yes, Nikos, yes. This—'

But the words died on her tongue, crushed back down her throat by the way that he suddenly stopped, his whole mood changing.

'No!'

His body stiffened, the dark head going back violently to look down at her with a new and devastating hostility, brutal rejection blazing in his eyes.

'No!' he said again, more forcefully this time.

The hands that had held her close were now moving her

away from him, setting her aside with cold precision. The fingers that had tangled in her hair were tugged free with a speed and roughness that brought pinpricks of tears to her eyes, though she was too stunned, too bewildered by the sudden change in mood to have even the energy needed to let them fall.

She couldn't find the strength to speak, either. Shock deprived her of her voice, so that even though she opened her mouth twice to try to protest she had to close it again when all she managed was an embarrassing croak. Stunned, she could only stand and watch in blank bewilderment as Nikos adjusted the fit of his jacket that her clutching fingers had knocked askew, smoothed his hands over his hair to bring it back into sleek order rather than the wayward tangle she had made of it.

And then, to her total consternation and horror, he actually checked his watch once again.

'Your time is almost up. You have just fifty seconds left,' he declared with flat detachment, completely devoid of emotion. 'Was there anything else that you wanted to say before you leave?'

CHAPTER THREE

HE SHOULD NEVER have touched her, Nikos told himself. Never been such a damn fool as to bridge the gap between them, do something as crazy as to put his finger on her face, feel the softness of her skin underneath his.

He should never have let himself get close enough to her to catch the scent of her skin, the clean softness of her hair.

Just a couple of steps forward was all it had taken. And, with the electrical sting of response to the moment their hands had touched around the glass still sizzling up his arm, he had already been halfway towards the madness of arousal that she had always been able to spark in him so instantly in the past.

And still could, damn it, it seemed.

He had spent the last five years trying to put her part in his life behind him, out of his mind. He had managed to get the taste of her out of his mouth and now it was right back there, sensual, intoxicating, driving him insane.

He had to be insane. How the hell else could he have let her get to him so far, so fast?

One touch and he had been right there, back in the maelstrom of searing hunger that tightened his throat, made his heart pound in his chest, made him hot and hard and hungry in the space of a single devastating heartbeat.

Just the feel of the soft flesh of her cheek under his finger-tip had brought a memory, fast and dangerous as a bolt of lightning, of the way it had felt to have her naked, all that softness underneath him, warm and willing, yearning for his touch, his caress…opening to him…

Thee mou, no! He was not going down that dangerous path again, sensually enticing though it was.

'I repeat,' he said, injecting every ounce of control he possessed into the ruthless command of his voice, 'is there anything else that you want to say before you leave?'

Was there anything?

Sadie felt as if her head was spinning, reeling as if from the force of a sudden fierce blow.

Her shocked, numbed brain wouldn't focus, and all she could think of was the feeling of Nikos's arms around her, the pressure of his body against hers. Her heart was still thudding ferociously and the taste of him was still on her lips. And deep in her body the yearning hunger that had uncoiled in those few fraught, dangerous moments was still burning, still stinging at her senses and making her feel miserably restless with unfulfilled need.

The clamour of every aroused cell made her feel as if she was being assailed by some appalling fever. One that had her burning up in one moment and then shivering in wretched cold the next.

'Well?'

Nikos's tone was harshly impatient, and damn him if he didn't flick another glance at that hateful watch, driving home his message without needing to say another word.

'I…'

Still unable to collect her thoughts, Sadie resorted to desperate measures, giving her head a rough little shake in an attempt to clear it. The movement caught Nikos's attention, making him frown ominously.

'And what does that mean?' he questioned sharply. 'Is it supposed to be no, you have nothing more to say? Or no, you have no plans to leave? Because I can tell you that you may not have plans—but I certainly do. I have another appointment in fifteen minutes, and a business lunch and an afternoon conference call after that. I don't have time to waste standing here, waiting for you to make up your mind and realise that you've had your chance—you made your plea and you lost.'

'Lost?' Sadie echoed dejectedly, recollection of why she was here coming back to her in full—and leaving her feeling worse than ever at the realisation that Nikos was dismissing her for good, with no chance at all of saving their home for her family.

'There is no way that I am going to sell you Thorn Trees,' she heard him say now, confirming her worst suspicions. 'Or rent it to you. My plans for the house remain just as they were when you—'

'Oh, please!' Sadie broke in on him, the thought of going home and telling her mother that she had failed driving her to one last desperate attempt to get him to show some compassion. 'Please don't say that! You have to understand—there has to be something I can do for you.'

'And what makes you think that? What the devil could I want from you? Believe me, there is nothing—'

'But there must be!'

'Nothing.'

His tone warned her not to argue further. And the way he raked both hands through his hair, pushing it back into its sleek control, spoke of a ruthless determination to be back on track, ready for the next move, that next appointment. This one was over and he was done with her.

'But that—what happened just now—surely…?'

Her words died as she looked into his face and his expression told her the terrible truth.

'What happened just now?' Nikos echoed cynically, his burning gaze searing over her from the top of her ruffled dark head to the toes of her black patent shoes.

The look of dark contempt that filled it made her shiver, feeling as if a much needed protective layer of skin had been stripped from her body, leaving her raw and exposed, frighteningly vulnerable.

'And what makes you think that what just happened had anything to do with anything?'

'But—you… I thought…'

Her tongue seemed to tangle up on itself, tying itself in knots so that she couldn't get the words out.

'You thought…?' Nikos prompted harshly when she fought with herself, trying to speak.

'I thought that that—that when you…'

When you kissed me. She just couldn't make herself say it. She knew that she would give herself away if she did. She had thought—had *hoped*—that the way he had kissed her so passionately meant that he still felt some trace of something for her. That, if nothing else, at least he was still attracted to her. And she had little doubt that that hope, that illusion—because his face made it plain it *was* an illusion—would show in her voice if she said anything more.

'When I kissed you?' Nikos drawled mockingly. 'Is that what you mean? So tell me, my sweet Sadie, just what did you think was happening? What do you think that was?'

'I—' Sadie tried to begin, but he ignored her stuttering attempt at speech and talked across her quite deliberately.

'Did you think it was warmth? Was that it? Or perhaps affection? Or perhaps…'

He actually had the nerve to stop, appear to consider, even

look suitably surprised, when deep down inside she knew damn well that the brute wasn't surprised at all but had been aiming for this right from the start.

'*Thee mou*, you didn't think it was *love*, did you?'

If she'd found it hard to speak before, then now Sadie found it absolutely impossible. She could feel the hot colour flaring in her cheeks and knew that her furiously embarrassed reaction had given her away completely.

'Then I'm sorry—'

'No, you're not!' Sadie broke in, finding her voice at last in the strength of the wave of anger that swept over her. 'You're not sorry at all. And I know it wasn't—wasn't anything like love.'

It couldn't have been. There was no way anyone could switch on love like that and then immediately turn it off right away.

'It certainly wasn't,' Nikos confirmed coldly.

'So what was it?'

Cruelty? Deliberate manipulation? Some sort of hateful test?

'Isn't it obvious?' Nikos questioned softly. 'I couldn't help myself.'

He'd shocked her there. It wasn't at all the answer she'd expected. But he'd anticipated her response and knew that he had her when her head went back in amazement, green eyes opening wide. A smile that did nothing to light up his face and had no effect at all on the coldness of his eyes flickered across his beautiful mouth as he noted her response.

He paused just long enough for his words to sink in and hit home before moving in for the kill.

'Lust will do that,' he declared, making sure that his words were totally clear. 'You always spoke to my most basic masculine nature—my libido—you still do. I find it hard to keep my hands off you.'

'Is that supposed to be a compliment? Because if it is you need to work on your technique.'

But Sadie's sarcasm, her attempt to hit back, simply bounced off Nikos's impenetrable hide without, apparently, even leaving a mark.

'Lust I can handle,' he went on, as if she had never spoken. 'It's something I can decide to indulge or not as I choose.'

'And you—decided to indulge it just now when you *pawed* me—'

'Not pawed, Sadie,' Nikos corrected, shaking his head almost as if in sorrow at her interpretation of his actions. 'I do not paw women. And if I had then you would not have responded as you did.'

'I—' Sadie tried to protest, but the sudden rush of confidence to speak seemed to have deserted her.

'If you want the truth,' Nikos continued, 'I wanted to know if you tasted the same. And you do.'

'Taste?'

It was the last thing she had expected.

'You still taste *exactly* the same.'

Nikos's mouth twisted on the words.

'I may not have recognised it before, but I see what it is now—the taste of lies and deceit—the taste of betrayal.'

Sadie flinched inwardly as he flung the words in her face. She wished she could deny them, throw her refutation right back into his dark, contemptuous face. But how could she when deep down she knew that they were nothing but the truth? She'd been forced to betray him, but he had planned his own betrayal with cold-blooded cruelty and with no one twisting his arm up behind his back—emotionally, at least. It had all been precisely what he had wanted all along.

'It wasn't exactly as you think. But I don't suppose you want to hear about that, do you?'

'You're damn right I don't. In fact, I do not want to hear another single word from you.'

'But the house…' Despair forced her to say it, pushing the words from her mouth when she just wanted to keep quiet and get out of there with some shreds of dignity intact. But she had her mother and her little brother to think of, and she couldn't let them down.

'Gamoto!' Nikos flung up his hands in a gesture of total exasperation. 'How many times do I have to tell you that I will not sell you Thorn Trees? Nor will I rent it to you—not at any price. Not if you were the last person on earth.'

'But there must be some arrangement we can come to! Surely there's something I can do—anything…'

The words shrivelled and died when she saw the fiendish light in his eyes and knew that she had made a terrible mistake.

'And exactly what sort of services did you have in mind? What exactly are you offering…?'

'Not that! Never!' Sadie flung at him, seeing the way his dark and cruel mind was going. 'If you really think that I'd sell myself…I'd rather die!'

'That was not the impression you were giving a few minutes ago,' Nikos returned, his voice sounding soft and silky but with an effect as brutal as a sharp stiletto sliding in between her ribs to stab at her heart. 'Then it was *Oh, Nikos—yes, Nikos…*'

'And you fell for it, didn't you?'

The words had flashed from her mouth before she had time to consider if they were wise or even safe. She only knew that she couldn't take any more of this black mockery. Of the appalling insults he was tossing in her direction with almost every word that came out of his mouth.

'You really thought that all you had to do was to touch me—kiss me—and I would be putty in your hands.'

'You were. That is exactly how you behaved.'

'I made it *seem* as if I was but you're pretty easy to fool. All I had to do was to let you cop a feel…'

The way that his black brows snapped together in a furious frown made her heart lurch in panic, cutting her words off short. Deciding hastily that it was probably safer not to think about the real reason why he looked so furious, instead she opted for a less contentious option and flashed him a mocking smile.

'Ask someone to translate,' she suggested wickedly.

'No translation necessary, believe me,' Nikos flung back, cold as ice. 'None at all. But if you think that that was what was happening then you are the one in need of an interpretation. And a reality check.'

'Oh, yes?'

'Oh, yes. If you think that all it takes is a flash of those stunning green eyes or a wiggle of your sexy little behind, then you really don't know me at all.'

'It felt—' Sadie began, but Nikos cut in on her, bringing one long-fingered hand down in a slashing gesture to emphasise his interruption.

'I was fool enough to go that way once before and I have no intention of ever putting my head into the noose all over again.'

'And you've made us pay for it ever since!'

Sadie was beginning to feel as if she was on some dangerous emotional rollercoaster. And it was all her own fault. After all she'd started this, with the pretence that she'd only been playing him along.

Playing him along—hah! That would be the day. She hated to admit it, even to herself, but the truth was that she *had* been putty in his hands. One kiss, one caress, and she had lost all grip on her sanity and been spun into a world of hot sensation and even hotter need. At least she had had the sense to realise that those casually tossed compliments—stunning green eyes and sexy little behind, indeed!—were not meant at all. They were just the practised flattery of a consummate womaniser. He probably rolled them out to whichever woman he happened to be with, changing the colour of their eyes where appropriate of course.

'You've had five years of taking your revenge. Haven't you done enough, had enough?'

'If you want the truth, then the answer is no,'

It was a flat, hard statement, his tone as harshly unyielding as his face, and when she looked into the deep pools of his eyes she saw no spark of warmth, no hint of humanity. Instead they were as cold and unresponsive as ice, his opaque, blanked-off stare shocking and frightening.

'What more can you have? There's nothing left. My father's dead—his fortune, his company are yours. Isn't that enough for you?'

'No, it is not.'

Nikos's golden eyes flicked over her face, catching and locking with her furious gaze just for one moment. Then he looked away again, heavy lids coming down to cut him off from her.

'I thought it was, but now I find it just won't do. It isn't enough. It doesn't give me the satisfaction that I wanted. I need to find some other way of making sure of that.'

And then she knew. With a terrible, sinking sense of despair she realised just what was going on here. Nikos Konstantos had always been determined to have his revenge for the way that Edwin had ruined his family. He had worked for that and for nothing else all the five years since she had last seen him. He'd taken the Carteret name, the Carteret business and stamped them into the mud, drained them of every last penny they possessed. He was even prepared to take the family home from them and throw her and her mother and little George out into the street.

And she had done the worst thing possible, made the most terrible mistake imaginable, by coming here to plead with him for a chance.

Because that had given Nikos one more chance to exact revenge on the member of the family he had the most personal reasons to hate. The one that he hadn't yet crushed beneath his heel and laughed in triumph as he did so.

He hadn't truly had his revenge on Sadie herself. Until now. And now it was strictly personal and totally ruthless. This wasn't about the house or the past except as it pitted the two of them against each other. This was the last part that would make his campaign of revenge complete.

He had her in his sights and he wasn't letting go.

'And the way you've found is by making sure that my family don't have a home to live in. How can you live with that on your conscience?'

'No problem.'

Nikos's shrug dismissed the question as being of no importance to him whatsoever. He didn't care and he had no intention of caring.

'I live with it as easily as you and your father could walk away from the devastation you made of my life—and my family's.'

'And you think that gives you the moral high ground? You were pretty damn good at playing games at that time, if I remember rightly.'

'Not games, Sadie.'

Nikos shook his head, his expression almost sorrowful, but Sadie knew that sorrow was the furthest thing from what he was feeling. He might hide it well but she knew that deep inside he was probably taking a cruel delight in tormenting her like this, having her with her back to the wall, nowhere to run.

'Believe me, I was serious. Deadly serious.'

'Oh, yeah, deadly serious about perpetuating that damn family feud. And look what that did to you. It almost ruined your family.'

'Almost,' Nikos echoed with deadly emphasis. 'Almost—

but it did not actually ruin us, did it? Not totally. And now the shoe is very definitely on the other foot.'

'As I'm only too well aware,' Sadie muttered belligerently.

She wondered what would happen if she told Nikos that the only reason that *'almost'* was even there was because of her. Because of the choice she'd made.

He'd probably never believe her. The mood he was in, he wasn't going to listen to anything she said.

'So this is checkmate, is it?' she went on. 'You must know that I can't leave it like this—without persuading you to let us stay in Thorn Trees....'

'That isn't going to happen,' Nikos stated with cold obduracy.

'So what do I do?'

Once more those powerful shoulders under the superbly tailored jacket lifted in an unfeeling and dismissive shrug.

'You said you were prepared to do anything to get what you wanted,' he drawled heartlessly. 'Turn those wiles that you were using earlier on someone else and you might have more success with someone who doesn't know you as well as I do.'

'Wiles...' Sadie spluttered in furious indignation. He really thought that she had set out to seduce him as a way to manipulate him into giving her what she wanted. 'How dare you...?'

But Nikos ignored her angry interjection.

'Find yourself another rich man and beg him to give you a chance to earn the price of the house. He might not find the offer so distasteful—his standards may not be as high as mine.'

Sadie gritted her teeth against the need to refute the implications of that cynical *'earn,'* though her fingers twitched sharply at her side with the urge to lash out and swipe that cold sneer from his arrogant face. Whatever momentary satisfaction it would bring—and it would be very satisfying—it would also make things so much worse and only succeed in angering Nikos even further.

'And if I did then you would only put the price up higher and higher each time.'

Nikos's smile was pure cold evil. The smile of the devil.

'How well you understand me, *glikia mou*. And, knowing me as you do, I am sure that you will recall that once I have made up my mind on a matter then I never change it. No matter what the temptation.'

And he had made up his mind on this, so it would be like battering her head against a brick wall if she continued to try to persuade him.

'And now, as you have had more than twice the amount of time allotted to you, I really would prefer it if you left immediately.'

Striding across to the door, Nikos pulled it open and stood pointedly, waiting for her to leave.

'I am sure that both of us would prefer to avoid the publicity that my calling Security might create.'

Knowing Nikos, Sadie recognised when she had come to the end of the road and there was nowhere else she could go. Defeat was staring her in the face and the only thing left to her was to accept it with as much dignity as she possibly could. Though the thought of going home and telling her mother…

Putting her head up high, stiffening her back and straightening her shoulders, she forced her feet to take her towards the door he had indicated. She had fully determined that she wouldn't say another word. That she wouldn't show him any weakness. She wouldn't even look at him. But somehow as she had to pass him her footsteps faltered, and in spite of her determination her reluctant gaze was drawn to his dark, stunning face, meeting the icy glare of those golden eyes.

'Is there nothing I can do…?' she began and knew her mistake as she saw his face harden even more, hooded eyes closing off from her.

'Yes,' he said coldly, unbelievably. 'The one thing you can do is go home and start packing—I want you out by the end of the week.'

It was the final blow, but at least his vicious tone was enough to stiffen her resolve.

'I'll do that,' she flung at him, refusing to let him see the terrible sense of defeat that was tearing at her soul.

'I'd appreciate it.'

Another couple of strides and she was beyond him, out of the room at last and marching straight down the long, soulless corridor, staring straight ahead.

She'd taken it better than he'd thought, Nikos admitted as he watched her go. Just for a moment there he had suspected that she was going to show him that she meant her declaration that she would do *anything* and turn back to him, coming close with smiles and deliberate kisses in an attempt to seduce him into giving her what she wanted.

And if she had done just that? The way his heart kicked and his body tightened gave him his answer.

Gamoto! Was he really going to let her walk out of his life once again, just as she had done five years before? With the taste of her still on his lips, with his body still in the grip of the burning arousal that just that one kiss had sent flaring through him, he knew that the answer was no. For almost five years he had tried to put this woman out of his mind and now, after less than an hour in her company, he knew why he had never fully managed to do it.

He still wanted her.

He wanted her like hell, in the way that he had never wanted any other woman in his life. And even the knowledge of the vile way she had behaved, the way she'd used an e-mail message to tell him she was backing out of their marriage— less than twenty-four hours before the ceremony—the cold-voiced rejection that she'd tossed down the stairs, couldn't erase the yearning hunger that plagued his senses. Watching the sway of her hips, the swing of the glossy dark hair as she walked away from him, he found he was actually considering calling her back, offering to renegotiate.

'You've had five years of taking your revenge. Haven't you done enough, had enough?'

The echo of her angry voice, just moments before, sounded inside his head. And his own answer came back at him fast, forcing him to face the truth.

'I thought it was, but now I find it just won't do. It isn't enough. It doesn't give me the satisfaction that I wanted. I need to find some other way of making sure of that.'

When Edwin Carteret had died, he'd thought he was done with the whole, hateful family. He'd clawed back every last penny of the fortune that had been taken from them and doubled it. He'd taken every asset the Carterets had owned—Thorn Trees being the last on the list—and seen his hated enemy reduced to total bankruptcy and ruin. To the black despair that his father had known and had barely even recovered from now. And he had thought that it was enough.

But one meeting with his nemesis in the seductive form of Sadie Carteret had brought that belief crashing down around him. Now at last he could put his finger on the feeling of restlessness and dissatisfaction that had plagued him in recent months. Before then he had been working too hard, barely even raising his eyes from his desk, from the files of stock market dealings, the takeover details and investments that had brought him to where he was now. It could never be enough because he hadn't dealt with the one remaining insult the Carterets had dealt him. Only this time it wasn't 'the Carterets' he had in his sights, but one member of that family in particular.

This time it was personal. Personal between him and seductive, manipulating Sadie Carteret.

And by coming here today Sadie had handed him just the
weapon he needed. She was desperate to get her hands on her
ancestral family home. Almost as desperate as he was to get
his hands on her silken skin, her feminine curves. To have her
under him in his bed once more. And the way she'd responded
to his kiss had left him in no doubt that she still felt the passion that had brought them together in that one explosive
weekend that had just been enough to awaken his appetite,
never enough to sate it.

She would do anything she could to get Thorn Trees, she
had said. Well, now he'd see how far she was prepared to go
to do just that. If things went the way he planned, then she
would get the damn house, and he could find the satisfaction
he needed and get Sadie Carteret out of his system once and
for all. In the most enjoyable way.

For a moment he thought about calling her back, and then
paused, shaking his head as he rethought. If he sent a message
down in the executive lift then she would get it before she left
the building.

Kicking the door shut, he went back to his desk and
reached for pen and paper.

The long, long corridor ahead of her blurred and danced as
Sadie fought with the tears that burned at her eyes, but this time
she was not looking back, she told herself. Not a single glance.
Even when it seemed to be an extraordinarily long time before
she finally heard the door to Nikos's office bang shut behind her.

Somehow she made it to the lift, and only once inside did
she let herself collapse back against the wall, her whole body
sagging limply and her head dropping forward as her eyes
closed. It was some moments before she could even think of
pressing the button for the ground floor.

She'd tried her best, given it her best shot. And she'd failed. Nothing, it seemed, could prevail against the black, brutal hatred that Nikos had let fester for all these years. Nothing could change him, restore him to the man he had once been. The man who had stolen her heart. The man she had been going to marry.

No.

Shaking herself roughly, she snapped her head up sharply, forcing herself to face facts once and for all.

She had to stop deceiving herself. That Nikos was a fantasy, a deception—a lie. The Nikos she had loved had never truly existed; he had simply been playing with her, manipulating her until he got exactly what he wanted. If her father hadn't moved in to protect her then the end result could have been far worse than it had. And it had been terrible enough.

The lift came to a halt, the doors sliding open, and Sadie pushed herself into motion, now desperate to get away, to be free of the tainted atmosphere of hatred.

It was as she crossed the wide, marble-floored foyer that she heard the beeping sound from her mobile phone. A text message. She knew who it would be from even before she had taken it from her bag, though the sight of 'New message from Mum' on the screen almost made her switch it off and not look.

But that would be the coward's way out. She had to face her family and let them know that she had failed some time. Taking a deep breath, she pressed the 'view' key.

How did you get on? her mother asked, as Sadie had known she would. *Have you got good news? Can we stay?*

Standing in the middle of the foyer, Sadie could only stare at the tiny screen until the backlighting blinked off and the whole thing went black. How was she going to do this? What could she say to soften the blow?

'Miss Carteret?'

It took a moment or two to register that the voice was speaking to her. That the receptionist she had talked to earlier had come up behind her and was now trying to get her attention.

'Excuse me, Miss Carteret, I have a message.'

'A message?'

Sadie stared blankly at the folded sheet of paper the other woman held out to her.

'From who?'

But even as she asked the question she knew there could only be one person who could have sent it. Only one man who could have dashed off the note and had it brought down to her in the executive lift, so it had caught up with her before she left the building.

Nikos. Just the thought of his name made her hand shake as she reached for the note.

'Thank you.'

She barely noticed the receptionist move away, her attention closely focussed on the piece of paper she held. After the way she had left Nikos upstairs, the brutal harshness of that final 'nothing', this was the last thing she had expected. He had been adamant that he was not going to help her, so why…?

Her fingers fumbled with the note as she unfolded it, tension blurring her vision as she tried to focus.

The note had neither greeting nor signature, but it didn't need one. There was no mistaking Nikos's dark, slashing scrawl. Just four brief words, dashed off in haste, and the sight of them made Sadie blink hard in bewilderment and confusion.

Cambrelli's 8:00 p.m. Be there.

Be there.

It was a blunt decree, a command that she would be wise to obey—or risk the consequences.

Be there.

And Cambrelli's. Dear heaven, but the man knew how to stick the knife in. Cambrelli's was the small Italian restaurant he had taken her to on their very first date.

Rebellion rose hotly in Sadie's heart. Who the hell was this man that he could issue such an order and expect to have it obeyed? Her fingers tightened on the paper, the impulse to crumple it into a ball and toss it away from her almost overwhelming. She was damned if she...

But even as she lifted her hand to do so, common sense reasserted itself and froze the defiant gesture. What was she thinking of? She knew exactly who this man was.

He was Nikos Konstantos, and he was in the position of having every command he issued obeyed at once, without any hint of a question. He also held all the cards very tightly in his hands.

'And, knowing me as you do, I am sure that you will recall that once I have made up my mind on a matter then I never change it.'

The words that Nikos had flung at her sounded so clearly inside her head that she almost believed that the man himself had come up behind her and spoken them out loud.

He had sworn that he would not help her and made it plain that every one of her entreaties had fallen on totally stony ground.

And yet...

Her gaze went back to the note in her hand as she smoothed it out and read over once again.

Cambrelli's 8:00 p.m. Be there.

She didn't know what it meant, but it seemed that Nikos had tossed her some kind of lifeline. It wasn't much but it was all she had, and she would be a fool not to grab at it while she could.

The receptionist was still hovering close at hand, obviously waiting for an answer. Glancing down at her phone, reading the message from her mother again, Sadie drew in a deep breath and came to a decision.

'Tell Mr Konstantos that I will meet him as arranged.'

CHAPTER FOUR

CAMBRELLI'S RESTAURANT HAD changed very little in the past five years. It was perhaps a little cleaner and brighter—they had obviously put a fresh coat of paint on the walls—but not much else had altered.

There were the same dark wood tables and chairs, some in small booths with red fake leather banquettes on either side, the same red-and-white checked tablecloths, the same candles stuck into empty wine bottles on each table, with wax dripping down the neck and over the label. She was sure that there were even the same rather worn and faded posters on the walls. One of the Colosseum in Rome and one of St Mark's Square in Venice. It was like stepping back in time and reliving a small part of her life.

If only she really could do that, Sadie thought as she followed the waiter to one of the booths near the back of the room, well away from the window, she noted. If only she could be arriving here as a rather naive twenty year old, still at university, her head in a whirl of excitement and her feet barely seeming to touch the ground as she headed for a date with the most exciting man she had ever met. Anticipating the most wonderful night she had ever known.

And it had been just that. That night and the days, the

months that had followed had been the happiest, the most glorious times Sadie had ever known. But if it was at all possible, if she really could go back in time, then she would grab hold of her younger self, try to shake some sense into her.

'Poor stupid little fool,' she muttered to herself, the bitterness of memory pushing the words from her mouth in spite of the fact that she wasn't really speaking to anyone.

'I beg your pardon, *signorina?*'

The waiter had heard her, and paused in his progress across the room to glance at her questioningly.

'Oh—sorry—nothing…'

She had to get a grip on herself, Sadie thought, managing an embarrassed half-smile. The stress of the day and anxiety about the evening ahead was getting to her and making her control of her tongue slip slightly. She needed to have her thoughts and her feelings totally under control.

But oh, how she wished that someone had taken charge of her younger self. That they had warned her not to trust Nikos, not to believe a word he said. Better that she should have faced the inevitable disillusionment then, before their affair had truly begun, rather than go through the whole terrible process of falling hopelessly and mindlessly in love and then being bitterly disappointed. The appalling sense of loss and betrayal had been all the worse because of the wonder and joy that had gone before.

But of course then she wouldn't have believed anyone who had tried to convince her that Nikos was not what he seemed. She wouldn't have listened to a single person—probably not even herself if she had managed to appear to give a warning message. At twenty years old she had been naive, gullible, and totally starry-eyed, and she would have thought that it would be well worth a broken heart at the end if she could only have that night.

She had never expected it to last anyway. She had only ever

thought that she would have that one night, one date. At the end of the evening she had fully expected that Nikos would take her home, say goodnight, and that would be that. She had been overjoyed, and unable to quite believe it, when he had asked to see her again—and again.

'Good evening, Sadie.'

Sadie had been so lost in her thoughts that she hadn't noticed they had reached the booth. It was already occupied, she realised, as in the shadowy darkness Nikos rose to his full height and faced her across the table.

This was not the man she had confronted in his office earlier that day. This Nikos was not the sleek suited businessman who headed the Konstantos Corporation. Instead he was darkly devastating in a soft black shirt, open at the neck with no tie, and worn black denim jeans that hugged the lean hips, the narrow waist that was emphasised by a heavy leather belt.

And just what was the message he intended her to read into that? Or was she reading too much into it because she had spent so long worrying about what she should wear herself— opting for a pair of smart black trousers with a deep red shirt and loose jacket so that she neither looked as if she had dressed up or down for this meeting? She was too acutely sensitive to the hidden clues in what Nikos had chosen to wear.

'Won't you sit down?'

The pointed question brought home to her the fact that she had been standing, still and silent, staring at him as if she had never seen him before in her life while he waited with carefully controlled patience for her response.

'Thank you.'

It was as she sank into the seat directly opposite him that she recalled how she had once been told that when eating out in a restaurant Greek men usually seated themselves with their backs to the wall, their guest facing them. That way the host could see everything that was going on, the coming and going in the main body of the restaurant, but their companion's attention was forced to be concentrated solely on them.

Not that Nikos's attention seemed to be anywhere else other than on her. Those bronze eyes were fixed on her face in a way that made the tiny hairs at the back of her neck lift in the uncomfortable reaction of a wary cat, faced with a threatening intruder into its space.

'So you came,' Nikos commented when the waiter had handed them menus and left them to decide on their meals.

'Of course I came. As you knew I would have to. I had no other choice. Not unless I wanted to stay at home and pack, as you'd already ordered me to do.'

'Not ordered. It was the logical next step if things stayed as they were,' Nikos corrected softly, earning himself a sideways glare that Sadie hoped made it clear that she was not in the least convinced by the apparent conciliatory tone in his voice.

There was no way that he was here to do any peace-making. Why should he when he held all the cards in his hands—and most of them were aces?

'And I suppose you are going to claim that you didn't order me to meet you here?'

'I merely invited you. So, what would you like to eat?'

Nothing. Sadie felt that she would be unable to swallow a single mouthful. Besides...

'Did you really invite me out for a meal?'

Nikos glanced up from his study of the menu, one black brow slightly lifted in mocking enquiry.

'Why else would we be in a restaurant, with menus to choose from?'

Because he wanted to prove that he had so much power over her that he could say jump and she would ask how high. Because he wanted to emphasise, by choosing this particular restaurant, just how very different things were now from the way they had been in the past, when they had been here together before.

'And why are we in this particular restaurant? Why here and nowhere else?'

'Because I know you like it here.'

If she didn't know better, she might almost believe in the innocence in his eyes, his voice. But she had no doubt that it was more than that. Nikos Konstantos never did anything without considering all possible outcomes and planning for the one that was exactly what he wanted.

'I liked it once,' she said coldly, pointedly. 'My tastes have changed since then.'

'Mine too,' Nikos drawled cynically.

So how was she supposed to take that? Was he, like her, thinking of the first meal they had eaten here? She hadn't known who he was then. Only that she had fallen for the most devastatingly handsome and attractive man she had ever met. If she had known would she have been more careful, more on her guard? Maybe even held back and never agreed to go out with him?

If she had then things would have been so much easier. She would never have become tangled up in Nikos's schemes—and those of her father. She would never have become a pawn in their hateful feud, never been used by each of them against the other. Because that had been all she was to them. A weapon which they could use to inflict as much damage on the other as possible.

'I understand that the calamari here is very good—unless you prefer—'

'What I'd prefer...' Sadie put in sharply, having foolishly let her eyes wander over the menu so that she spotted the delicious shrimp dish she had eaten that first time she had been here. She could almost taste it in her mouth, the memory was so clear and devastating. 'What I'd *prefer* is that you tell me exactly why I'm here and what you want from me.'

'Some wine first?' Nikos returned imperturbably, lifting one hand to summon the waiter.

The response was immediate, as of course it always was with Nikos. He only had to make the slightest gesture, look as if he might need something, and there was always someone there, right at hand, ready to provide whatever he needed.

But the presence of the waiter and his enquiring glance in her direction, the way he brandished his notepad and pen, meant that she couldn't pursue the topic she wanted with him standing there listening. Feeling cornered, with her back against the wall, she snatched up the menu again and chose a pasta dish completely at random, only wanting the man to be gone so that she could confront Nikos and find out just what was going on.

'I don't for one moment believe,' she began as soon as they were alone again, 'that you have invited me here simply to spend an evening together and eat pasta—however good it might be.'

'You're right…'

Nikos set his own menu aside and folded his hands together on the tabletop. The movement made a sudden flash of gold catch the light from the candle flame, and Sadie felt her heart thud just once, hard and sharp against her ribs, as she realised that she had no idea whether Nikos was married or if there was a woman in his life.

Someone to replace her.

Outside a heavy rumble of thunder announced the fact that a storm was approaching. Sadie noted it with only half her mind, the rest of her attention focussed on those long, strong, tanned fingers resting on the red and white checked cloth. Fingers where she now saw the gold was just a signet ring, worn on Nikos's right hand. At the realisation her breath escaped her in a rush. Breath that she hadn't even been aware of holding in.

'I haven't just invited you here to spend the evening with me. I asked you to meet me because I wanted to offer you a job.'

'A job?'

And now the waiter was back with the wine, interrupting them again. Was Nikos really making a particular thing about checking the label, having the bottle opened, tasting the small amount the waiter poured into his glass? Or was it just that it seemed that way to her, with every long drawn out second seeming to grate more on her already overstretched nerves, making her want to scream or make some protest. Instead she had to settle for waiting, her back tense, teeth digging into the softness of her bottom lip, until he had nodded his satisfaction and indicated that the waiter should pour her a drink.

'No, thanks,' Sadie put in hastily, pressing her hand over the top of her glass. She needed to keep a clear head until she found out just what Nikos was up to. If he pressed her...

Nikos took her decision with surprising equanimity, sipping appreciatively at the rich red liquid in his own glass, once again taking his time before he moved the conversation on at all. Sadie couldn't stand the waiting any longer.

'What sort of a job?' she demanded when the silence had stretched out just too long to bear. 'Why would you want to employ me? And what makes you think that I would ever want to work for you?'

'You did,' Nikos told her coolly, taking another swallow of his wine.

'I never!'

'Oh, yes, you did.'

And when she frowned in blank incomprehension, he shook his head slightly, as if in disbelief.

'What a very short memory you have, Miss Carteret. What-ever happened to "There must be some arrangement we can come to! Surely there's something I can do—anything"? *Any-thing,*' he added, with soft menace and deadly emphasis.

Recalling the interpretation he had put on that *'anything'* earlier that day, Sadie suddenly wished she had accepted some of the wine. Right now it might ease the painful knot of tension tight in her chest, ease the uncomfortably jerky pound-ing of her heart. She knew she would do anything in her power to gain some extra time that her mother and George could spend in the home that meant so much to them. But did Nikos really mean…?

'What exactly did you have in mind?' she managed to croak, another rumble of distant thunder seeming to under-line the apprehension in her tone.

Once more Nikos took his time in replying, stony, hard eyes never leaving her face as he leaned back in his chair and seemed to consider his response. Not that he had any need to, Sadie re-flected. She had little doubt that he knew exactly what he was going to say and how it would affect her. She had the most un-comfortable feeling that she was as powerless as a puppet, with its strings dangling from the hands of a ruthless and cruel master.

'We'll come to that in a moment,' he said evenly. 'But first I want you to tell me exactly why you want the house so much.'

'Isn't it obvious?' Sadie hedged, unwilling to expose her mother's story to his pitiless gaze.

'Oh, yes, totally obvious.'

Could his tone get any more cynical?

'Young woman with no money, a not very successful busi-ness as a wedding planner…'

Seeing her start of surprise, he gave a tight smile.

'I make sure I keep up to date with what is happening to anyone I have had dealings with in the past.'

So how much did he know? The idea of being kept under surveillance like that when she hadn't known he was watching made her skin crawl.

That smile grew darker, more dangerous, the blaze of the candles reflected in the depths of his penetrating gaze.

'I always thought that it was something of a very black irony that someone who walked out on her own wedding just the day before it was due to take place should now make her living organising other women's "big days."'

Nikos's sensual mouth twisted on the words.

'But then the one thing I could never deny is that you always had that very special sense of style. When other people were paying, of course.'

'I had to do something to earn a living,' Sadie managed from between tight lips. 'And that at least was a way of using my design course.'

The one her father had paid for as a reward for doing as he asked of her. She wouldn't need it, Edwin had told her. After all, she was going to be a great catch—a very wealthy young woman now that he had seen off the opposition, which was the way he had described his takeover of almost everything the Konstantos family had owned.

But Sadie had known that she couldn't just sit around at home. For one thing, the atmosphere there between her parents had been so poisonous that it had been an endurance test simply to breathe the same air. And, for another, the last thing she had wanted to do was to consider the prospect of another suitor who would only want to marry her because of the huge inheritance that was going to come to her when her father died.

She'd been through that once. And once was more than enough.

'And it was something I could do from home.'

Nikos nodded slowly, turning the stem of his glass round and round in his tanned fingers.

'And of course Thorn Trees is a prestigious address from which to run a business that would attract society brides and their wealthy families.'

'But that isn't why I want to keep the house!'

A deliberately lifted eyebrow questioned her over-emphatic outburst.

'Then why would you want to live in a huge London mansion with—what?—seven bedrooms and an indoor pool? Preferably for free, or at the most for a tiny rent. So, tell me exactly why you need a house like Thorn Trees? Do you plan to sleep in each of the bedrooms on a different day of the week?'

'Oh, now you're just being ridiculous! Of course not! And I wouldn't be living there on my own.'

That had his attention. She could tell by the way his back stiffened, cold eyes burning into her as the swept over her face. Sadie felt she could also tell just what was going through his mind—clearly his 'keeping up to date' hadn't resulted in him finding out the story about her mother. At least that was one thing her father had done properly before he died.

But the waiter was back again, this time bringing their meals, and Nikos was forced to sit and wait—obviously burning up with impatience—to be served before he could find out more. The man barely had time to put the plates on the table before Nikos was waving him away, ignoring his questions as to whether there was anything else they wanted.

'Who?' he demanded, and Sadie allowed herself a moment or two to prolong the tension, knowing it would provoke him even more.

'Did you have to send him away like that?' she complained. 'I might have wanted some parmesan…'

A flick of Nikos's hand dismissed her protest as irrelevant and unimportant.

'*Who?*' he repeated.

'Well, not what you're thinking—so you can get your mind out of the gutter. Do you really think that I would ask you to finance my love life by providing a home for me and my lover?'

He wouldn't put it past her, Nikos acknowledged to himself. Sadie Carteret had had a liking for the good things of life, always provided someone else was paying. The way she had discarded him so quickly when his family had been ruined and he had lost his personal fortune had been proof of that. And of course she had deliberately distracted him so that her father could work behind the scenes, planning hostile takeovers, finding ways to bring the Konstantos empire down. She had even been prepared to sacrifice her own virginity to ensure that the destructive plan succeeded.

Beyond the windows, yet another distant rumble of thunder after what he assumed was the flash of lightning just seemed to underline the point of her corruption.

'Nothing would surprise me.'

'Well, for your information, I share the house with my mother and little brother.'

That was so unexpected that it seemed to hit like a blow between his eyes, making his head go back in shock, eyes narrowing assessingly. This was information he had not been given.

'You don't have a brother.'

The look Sadie turned on his was wide-eyed, innocent, sharply contrasting with the way that her chin came up and she faced him defiantly over the table.

'Well, that just goes to show that your amazing spy network isn't as good as you thought. For your information, I *do* have a brother—a little brother called George. He was born— He's not quite five.'

Five. Why did it seem that everything that had turned his life upside down had happened at the point not quite five years before? So her mother had been pregnant around the time when they had been together and planning to get married, or just after. And little George had been born into the maelstrom of action and reaction once her father's plan to bring down the house of Konstantos had been put into motion.

And of course in those months he had been focusing only on holding things together. On keeping the corporation from going under and taking his beleaguered father with it. At the time he had felt that if he thought about anything else, focussed on anything else, then the dark waves of total disaster would break over his head and he would definitely go down for the third time—and never come up again.

But the fact that she had a brother put a different complexion on the fact that Sadie wanted to keep the house. This George was so young that there was no way he could have ever been involved in anything the adult Carterets had planned and implemented against his family.

'I see,' he said, the words loaded with dark meaning. 'That explains why I never got to hear of it. So tell me…'

'No.'

Ridiculously buoyed up by the small triumph she'd had in putting him mentally onto the wrong foot for once, Sadie waved the hand that had picked up her fork to dig into her pasta to silence him.

'My turn.'

He might hold all the aces, but that didn't mean that she was going to let him get away with monopolising the conversation and treating the meal as if it was a trial for fraud with him as the counsel for the prosecution.

'I get to ask some questions too.'

Was that a grudging respect in his eyes, the inclination of

his head? Just the possibility gave her a little surge of confidence as she forked up a mouthful of her pasta.

'What questions?'

'Well, the obvious, for a starter. Like—you said you wanted to talk to me about a job. What sort of a job could I do for you? I mean—what need would you have of a wedding planner?'

'That really is asking the obvious,' Nikos commented. 'To plan a wedding, of course.'

The impact of his response hit home just in the moment that Sadie popped the forkful of pasta into her mouth and chewed. Too late she realised that she'd been in such a state of apprehension when she'd arrived at the restaurant that she'd blindly ordered her meal with an *arrabiata* sauce, instead of the one next to it on the menu. She loathed chillies, and this was heavily laced with them.

'A wedding?' she croaked through the burn in her mouth, tears of reaction stinging her eyes.

'Here…'

Leaning forward, Nikos poured a glass of water, held it out to her, watching as she gulped it down gratefully.

'You hate spicy food,' he said, when she finally started to breathe more easily. 'Particularly chillies.'

Did he remember everything about her? It was a scary thought.

'So why order something that you were going to hate?'

'It's almost five years. I might have changed—people do.'

'Obviously not that much,' Nikos drawled, his dry tone making her wonder if there was so much more than her reaction to the chilli sauce behind his comment. 'Would you like something else?'

'No—thank you.'

Any appetite she had had fled in the moment he had made that stunning announcement. But at least the impact of the chillies had disguised the fact that a lot—oh, be honest!—most of her reaction had been in response to his declaration. Her heart was still thudding from the shock of it, her thoughts spinning, whirling from one emotion to another and back again.

And none of the reactions was one that she really wanted to take out and examine in detail. Not here, not now. Not with Nikos lounging back in his chair, watching every move she made.

'Whose wedding?' she managed to croak. 'Are you telling me that you are getting married?'

Once more Nikos inclined his dark head in agreement.

'Who to?'

'I prefer not to say. One never knows when the paparazzi might be hanging around, looking for a story. I prefer that they do not find out about this just yet. I want to protect my fiancée.'

A protection he hadn't offered her, Sadie recalled with a stab of bitterness. Then he had been happy that the world should know about their engagement, their upcoming wedding. With the result that she had begun to feel she was living her life in a goldfish bowl, with a huge, powerful spotlight directed right at it all the time.

Which had made their final break-up into a media circus that had left her shattered and devastated.

'And you don't trust me?' she asked, as much to distract herself from the particularly vivid, particularly painful memories that had risen to the surface of her mind, no matter how much she tried to push them down.

'You will find out soon enough—when the time is right for you to know.'

It seemed that Nikos too had abandoned all pretence at having an appetite for his meal. His ignored sea bass was rapidly cooling on his plate as he focussed only on her.

'And of course when you are in Greece…'

'What?'

She couldn't have heard that right.

'No—wait a minute—back up a bit here. What was that? I thought you said… I'm not going to Greece!'

'Of course you are.'

Nikos's half smile was perfectly composed, totally in control.

'How else will you organise the wedding?'

'Your wedding?'

The croak in her voice was worse than the one inflicted by the bite of the chillies. She could hardly believe that she had heard anything right. Had he really said?

She couldn't… She *wouldn't!* How could he expect her to organise and arrange a wedding at which he—the man she had once been going to marry herself—would become someone else's husband? He couldn't ask it of her! It was too cruel. Too monstrous.

But the reality was that Nikos wasn't *asking.* He was simply stating a fact. As far as he was concerned this was what was going to happen. She was going to take on the arranging of his wedding—to his fiancée. Because he said so.

'No…'

It was all she could manage. Even after a long, shaken gulp of cooling water, her throat refused to allow her to say any more.

'I said that I had a job for you.'

'*This* is the job? This is what you brought me here to talk about?'

And what sort of twisted vindictiveness had driven him to bring her here, to the restaurant where they had shared their first meal together, and where, barely two months later, he had proposed to her in one of the other candlelit booths?

'Well, thank you for the offer, but I'm afraid I'm going to have to decline the commission. I can't go to Greece.'

And she couldn't possibly work with him on his plans to marry someone else.

'I'm afraid that you do not have that option.' Nikos's tone took his response to a place light years away from any real regret. In fact, it made it only too plain that the very last thing he was was sorry. 'This is not a job that you can turn down— or even stop to think about. Not if you really meant what you said when you told me you would do anything if I would just let you live in Thorn Trees.'

'So…' Sadie drew in a slow, deep breath and let it out again on a thoughtful sigh. 'This is your price for what I asked? I work for you—plan your wedding—and you'll allow me to stay in…'

'I'll allow your mother and brother to stay in the family home. For now,' Nikos put in, making it plain that his concern was only for them.

'What made you change your mind? Only this morning you were saying that you wouldn't even consider it.'

'Your mother played no part in what happened in the past. Neither did your brother. Because of that I am prepared to make some concessions for them.'

Which once again put the emphasis of what he was doing firmly on the personal, between Nikos and herself. And what he wanted from her was for her to organise this wedding for him and so rub her nose in the fact that he had not only moved on but totally replaced her in his life. The cruel sting of that thought made her wish again that she had let him pour her some wine. At least then she could have lifted her glass, sipped from it—even if she was only pretending to drink. She could have fiddled with the glass, hidden her face behind it, anything that would distract him from the hurt, the feeling of being at a loss, she knew must show in her face.

'But I don't know anything about Greek weddings—

you would do better with someone else, someone who knows all about—'

'I don't want anyone else. I want you.'

'Surely your bride-to-be will have some say in the matter?'

'My bride-to-be will leave things entirely in my hands.'

'Oh, she will, will she? What's this—you're reverting to type and determined to get yourself a sweet little innocent wife who daren't say a word against you.'

'Unlike the wife I would have had if I'd married you?' Nikos drawled cynically, swilling the rich red wine around in his glass before taking a long drink from it. 'No one could ever have described you as "sweet"—or "innocent."'

'But then you never really wanted to marry me in the first place,' Sadie flashed back, still fighting with the pain of her memories.

She'd been an innocent when he'd met her—still a virgin at twenty. But naively, crazily, head over heels in love, and thinking she was going to be married to the love of her life, she had thrown that special gift away, giving it to the man who she believed loved her but who had in fact just been using her cynically and cruelly as a way to get at her father.

'On the contrary...' Nikos countered. 'I wanted you very much indeed. So much so that I was out of my head with it.'

'So that's all I was to you—a mental aberration?'

She had needed the reminder of how ruthlessly he had behaved. He might have wanted her, all right, but only physically. And she had offered herself to him on a plate, pushing to anticipate their wedding vows.

It was that same night when she had discovered just what Nikos had really been up to when he had claimed he wanted to marry her.

'You certainly drove me crazy. Are you going to eat that?'

He nodded his dark head towards the plate of rapidly

cooling pasta that now was beginning to look nastily congealed and even more unappealing.

'No chance.'

Sadie gave an exaggerated shudder, and to her astonishment a smile flickered on Nikos's lips. Brief, barely there, but it did at least have a trace of real warmth, real amusement.

'I knew that would happen when you ordered it. Remembering how much you hate chillies…'

'Then why didn't you say something?' she demanded, causing Nikos to hold up his hands in front of himself in a gesture of appeasement.

'I also remember what you were like when anyone tried to tell you what to do,' he said dryly.

And for a moment, as their eyes met across the table, it was as if the years had fallen away and they were back on that very first date, with every part of their relationship brand-new and fresh. When they had both been just learning about each other and everything had seemed bright and clear, with so much potential lying ahead.

As the flickering candle-light played over Nikos's stunning face it emphasised shadows, showed up lines that she hadn't seen before. Lines that five years of experience had put on his face, under his eyes, around his mouth. But somehow the marks of time seemed only to enhance rather than reduce the powerful masculine appeal of his hard features. At this time of day his strong jaw was already shaded with the darkness of a day's growth of beard and, seeing it, Sadie suddenly had a rush of vivid, painful memory of just how she had loved the feel of that faint roughness against her skin when he kissed her, the lightly stinging response it had always left behind.

Nikos's eyes were dark, deep pools above the broad slash of his cheekbones, and his sensual mouth was stained faintly by the rich red wine he had just drunk, his lips still moist from it.

As their gazes clashed, froze, locked together with an intensity that made it seem as if the whole of the restaurant and everyone in it had faded into a hazy blur, the murmur of conversation blended together until it made a sound like the distant buzzing of a thousand bees—there, but making no real sense at all.

All the breath seemed to stop in her throat, making her lips part in an attempt to snatch in air that she had almost forgotten how to breathe. She felt as if she was drowning in those eyes, losing herself and going down for the third time as hot waters of sensuality swirled around her head, making her senses swim dangerously. Outside, in the darkened rainswept street, the lightning flashed again, but Sadie barely saw it. It was only when a growl of thunder made her jump that she came back to herself in a rush.

'Nikos...'

She barely knew she had spoken, only that the sound of his name had escaped on a breath that had somehow formed into the word. And when she looked around, with things coming back into focus again, she saw how she had actually put her hand out to him, trying to make contact. Her arm lay across the gingham tablecloth, her fingers stretched towards his, almost making contact.

In the space of a jolting heartbeat she knew what a mistake she had made. She saw the way the man before her blinked hard, just once, and when he opened his eyes again it was as if all trace of any emotion, any warmth, had been washed from them leaving them, opaque and cold as a pebble at the bottom of a mountain stream. With that blink the silent connection that seemed to have formed between was broken, shattered, and Nikos suddenly straightened up, reaching for his napkin and dabbing it to his mouth.

'Then we'll go. I've said what I wanted to say and you will need to get home and pack. We leave for Athens in the morning.'

'Leave…'

Indignation and exasperation burned away any last remaining shreds of the disturbing sensual response she had just felt, leaving her feeling uncomfortable and totally on edge.

'But I haven't said I'll come yet. You can't just—'

'There's nothing for you to say,' Nikos cut across her attempt to protest, pushing back his chair and standing up as he did so. 'It's make your mind up time, Sadie. You either pack to come with me to Greece in the morning—or you pack up everything for yourself, your mother and brother and leave Thorn Trees. So which is it to be?'

It was the reminder of her mother and George that decided the question, as Nikos had obviously intended it should. He had held out the offer to let them stay, but only on his terms. And those terms involved her going with him to Greece and working to arrange Nikos's wedding to his new bride.

'Your choice, Sadie,' Nikos prompted harshly when she still hesitated.

Which, of course, was no choice at all. There was only one thing she could say. Only one way she could keep her mother and George safe and happy. No matter what the personal cost to her.

'I'll come,' she said. 'It seems I have no choice.'

'None at all,' Nikos assured her. And the really disturbing thing was the total lack of any sort of triumph or satisfaction in his tone.

He had planned for just this result and things had worked out exactly as he intended. He had expected nothing else. Because he knew exactly where he had her—dancing on the end of the strings that he was holding, in total control of her life. And there was nothing she could do about it.

CHAPTER FIVE

'WE WILL BE preparing to land soon.'

Nikos's accented voice broke into Sadie's concentration, making her jump.

'You'll need to put that away.'

His gesture indicated the laptop on which she had been working ever since the private jet had levelled out on their flight to Athens, her attention totally focussed on the screen.

'What are you working on anyway?'

'Greek wedding customs—what else?' Sadie swivelled the machine round so that he could see the site she had been studying.

She had been glad to disappear into her need to concentrate on the reason she was on the plane in the first place. It had meant that she could try at least to ignore Nikos's long, lean form sprawled in one of the soft leather seats on the opposite side of the cabin.

But the truth was that her mind hadn't really been on her research. Instead, it had insisted on taking her back into the past, replaying scenes of the times she had spent with Nikos when the only wedding she had been planning had been her own. She had desperately needed a real distraction from that.

'I take it that you are planning a traditional wedding,

seeing as you have insisted on dragging me out to Greece with you?'

Nikos shrugged off the question with an indifferent lift of one shoulder.

'Have you even given your bride a choice? Or will you just dictate how things are to be?'

That brought his eyes to her face, coldly probing, as if he was trying to read what went on behind her eyes. And she could see the flash of something fierce and dark in their golden depths.

'Are you saying that this is how it was with you? That I dictated everything?'

'No.'

How could she claim that? He had insisted she should have everything exactly the way she wanted. It was her choice, he had told her, her wedding. She should choose everything. And as a result it had really been the way her father had wanted things, not her choice at all.

But then, of course, that had been because he had never truly meant to marry her. All the time Nikos had been planning on using her to distract her father while he and his family worked to ensure his downfall, the ruin of his company. It was only when she found out the truth that she had realised why he had been so unexpectedly easygoing, so unconcerned about having an Orthodox wedding.

'Of course you didn't dictate anything. Because nothing mattered enough to you to bother with that.'

'You couldn't be more wrong.'

Nikos's smile sent a shiver down her spine.

'Oh, of course, there was one thing.' She flung the response at him. 'I know only too well just what mattered to you. You wanted me in your bed and that was all.'

'And I had you there without too much trouble, as I recall. You practically threw yourself at me.'

She had played right into his hands there, Sadie admitted. At first determined that she would wait until her wedding night to give her virginity to the man she adored, she had completely lost her head just a short time before the big day. So she had hired a cottage, enticed Nikos away with her for a long weekend of blazing passion.

Instead it had turned into a dreadful time when her dreams had started to unravel and she had finally begun to learn the truth.

These were the memories that had plagued her as the plane sped towards Greece. Echoes of the time when Nikos, thinking she was asleep, had gone downstairs to answer a call on his mobile phone. But Sadie had only been dozing and, missing him, had crept down after him. Before she'd opened the door she'd caught a drift of his conversation and had stopped to listen. And what she'd heard had shattered her illusions and fantasies, making them tumble in pieces all around her.

'Don't worry,' she'd heard Nikos say, a thread of dark, cruel laughter in his voice. 'There is more than one way to skin this particular cat. When my ring is on his precious daughter's finger and she's part of the Konstantos family too, then Carteret will soon come to heel. We'll have him exactly where we want him.'

'It was what I wanted at the time,' she said now, matching Nikos with an equally dismissive shrug.

Somehow she managed to make her voice hard enough to conceal the way that her memories tore at her heart. She even added a curl of her lips, as if in contempt at her younger self.

'Don't forget I was naive and innocent then. I had nothing to compare you to.'

'Inexperienced, maybe—innocent, never,' Nikos scorned. 'You knew exactly what you were doing and you played your virginity as your trump card.'

'It wasn't like that!'

'No? So are you going to tell me what it *was* like? Are you going to claim that you were truly as crazily in love with me as you pretended to be?'

She was heading into dangerous waters here, Sadie told herself. If she admitted the truth, that she had adored him, that he had been her life, then he would want to know why she had turned on him as she had done. And she still had enough pride to want to hide from him just how much she knew of the way he had used her callously in his determination to bring down her family.

And she needed to tread carefully while Nikos was in total charge of the situation. For his own private reasons he was prepared to be unexpectedly generous. He was letting her mother and George stay in the house for now. But she was terrified that if she rocked the boat in any way he might change his mind. Just the memory of the way her mother's face had lit up when she had been able to give her good news last night was enough to keep a careful check on her tongue.

'*Crazy* would be a good way to describe it,' she hedged carefully. 'You were pretty hot back then, Nikos, and I was tired of being a virgin. But don't kid yourself that you were anything special.'

'Oh, I won't.' Nikos's response was darkly dangerous, the savage edge to it slashing like a cruel knife. 'Believe me, I never did. Now, are you going to switch that thing off or not?'

'Oh—sorry…'

Hastily, she closed down the site she had been studying, saving her notes before switching off the whole computer. Her movements clumsy, partly from haste and partly because of the burning intensity of his scrutiny, she shut it up and bundled it into the case on the floor beside her seat.

'I'll take that.'

Nikos leaned over to pick up the case.

'Oh, but…' Sadie tried to protest but he dismissed it with a gesture.

'The staff will see to our luggage and this will go with it. You will get it back when it's necessary. And what about your phone? Your mobile will need to be switched off.'

'Of course.'

The phone was in her bag, and as she pulled it out she saw that the words telling her she had a newly arrived text message were on the screen.

'It's from my mother. Can I just see this…?'

Another flick of his hand urged her to do just that and be quick about it, his impatience making her all fingers and thumbs as she checked her message.

It was a long one, and she had to scroll down to read it all. Then scroll back again to reread, not quite believing what she had seen.

'Sadie…'

Nikos's hand was held out towards the phone. He didn't quite click his fingers in impatience, but that mood was very much in the air as he waited for her to respond.

'But…'

Sadie's eyes were still on the text message.

'Mum says that she's had a letter from you—a courier delivery. And you…'

She had to spin round, had to look straight into Nikos's face to try to read his expression.

'Is this true? Have you really sent my mother written notification that she can stay in Thorn Trees for now?'

The answer was there in his face, in the swift, darkened glance that he directed briefly at the phone and then at Sadie once again.

'I instructed my solicitor to send a letter this morning.'

'But why?'

'I told you. Your mother and brother played no part in what happened in the past. It would be inhuman to take revenge on a child.'

Which once again brought a shiver of apprehension at the thought that revenge was in his mind at all.

She was here to organise his wedding, wasn't she?

'And this is in return for my helping to plan and arrange your wedding?'

The bronze eyes that met her questioning glance were cool and opaque, all emotion blanked out so that there was nothing to read, nothing to give her any help.

Nothing to ease that cold edge of uncertainty that had shivered down her spine.

'Our arrangement is that you will do a job for me. As long as you carry out that job to my satisfaction then your mother and brother will be able to stay in the house without harassment or upset. I have sent them a letter informing them of that.'

'Thank you!'

After the fear and uncertainty of the moment she had left his office only the day before the rush of relief was so great that it pushed aside all sense of restraint, driving her into instinctive action without a thought of the consequences. With her phone still in her hand, she bent forward, lifting her face to press a swift, light-hearted kiss on Nikos's lean cheek.

'Thank you!' she said again. Then froze as reaction hit home.

It had been meant to be light-hearted. Rationally, that was what she had told herself. But what thumped straight into her heart was a response that was very far from rational.

Just the scent of his body in her nostrils, the taste of his skin on her lips, the faint rasp of stubble breaking through the olive-toned flesh, went straight to her head like the most potent alcohol. Her mind swam, her vision blurring so that every other sense came into sharper focus. She couldn't stop herself from letting her tongue slip out to experience, very softly, the faintly salt taste of his skin, knowing in that moment such a sudden rush of memories and sensations that she felt as if the plane they were in had hit sudden violent turbulence that swung them up and down and from side to side until she was dizzy with shock and sensation.

She wanted to press herself up against the hard strength of his body, wind her arms up and around his neck, fingers tangling in the jet silk of his hair. She wanted to turn her head just an inch or more, so that it met with the warm temptation of his lips. She longed to deepen the taste of him as their mouths joined, opened…

She knew her mistake even before the thoughts had fully formed in her mind. She felt his sudden tension, the stiffening of that long body, the way his jaw tightened until his whole face was just one rigid mask of rejection, so cold and unyielding that it was almost like kissing the carved, immobile face of some marble statue. She felt as if her mouth must be bruised by slamming up against it.

'No!'

Nikos's response was sharp and violent. The swift jerk of his head repulsed her foolish gesture, and he wrenched himself away from her with a force that had her almost losing her balance. Instinctively, her hand went out to grasp at Nikos's arm for support, then immediately released it again as she felt the even more powerful rejection that stiffened it against her.

'I'm sorry!'

Somehow she managed to stay upright. But the fight for equilibrium in her mind was harder won as she struggled with the terrible sense of loss that seared through her with the force of a lightning strike. She had forgotten that Nikos had told her he was marrying someone else, that he was committed to another woman. It was no wonder he had reacted so forcefully to her impulsive response.

'That wasn't any sort of come-on—truly it wasn't. It was only a thank-you!'

Could the look he turned on her be any colder, any more distant? Was it possible that she could endure the icy contempt that seemed to strike with the force of an arctic blast and not shrivel under the force of it, crumpling where she sat?

'It won't happen again.'

'You're damned right it won't happen again.' Nikos turned on her in dark fury. 'If you thought that you could win me round to giving you whatever you want by seducing me then you couldn't be more wrong. I may have been caught that way before, but never again.'

'You were caught?' Sadie scorned. 'In my opinion it was exactly the opposite way round! I was the one caught in your trap. The one you hunted down. You could never have been caught because I'm not sure you ever intended to marry me. You simply wanted to use me in your damned family feud with my father.'

'Oh, I would have married you, all right,' Nikos tossed back, the words hitting her like a slap in the face. 'By then I was so completely obsessed with you that I would have done anything—however stupid—to have you in my bed. One night with you was not enough. Could never be enough. I would have put my head right back in the noose if only to have another one.'

What else had she expected? Sadie asked herself, struggling with the bitter pain that had put a taste like acid in her mouth. Had she really believed that Nikos would deny the accusation she had thrown at him? That he would claim—pretend—he had actually felt something for her? That he would even declare that he had loved her?

She'd known the real truth all along. Ever since her father

had enlightened her. And yet it still hurt so terribly, ripping great raw and bleeding holes in her heart.

'But not now,' she managed.

'Not now,' Nikos confirmed darkly.

'Of course you have a new fiancée now. A new lo…'

But her voice failed her then. There was no way she could form the word *love*. It didn't belong on her tongue and it seemed to have formed a cruel knot in her throat, so that she could barely manage to breathe.

'I will do my very best to create a wonderful wedding for you both.'

It was the only way she could thank him for the reprieve he had offered her and her family. The chance to try and make sure that her mother survived the upheavals in their life and maybe found a future to look forward to. The thought of her mother twisted on nerves deep inside her. She had made the best provision she could for Sarah, and that text at least made it seem that she was coping for now. But Sadie had never been away from home for more than a day since the truth about George had burst on the family. She could only pray that her mother would cope.

'When will I meet your fiancée?'

Or even get to know her name? It was the first time she'd ever taken on a commission with so little information and no chance to meet the bride-to-be. She had never encountered a set-up like this.

'You'll have all the information you need when the time is right.'

At that moment a bell sounded and a light came on over the seats, an indication that they should fasten their seatbelts. Immediately Nikos held out his hand, palm upwards.

'Phone…' he snapped, with an impatient beckoning gesture of the hand that was between them.

Her mind still half on her mother and George, Sadie blindly

followed the command that was in his rough, irritated voice. She had dropped her mobile phone into his upturned palm before it occurred to her to question what he wanted with it.

'Hey—hang on…!'

But she had spoken too late. Even as she opened her mouth Nikos's long fingers had snapped shut over her phone, and without another word he dropped it swiftly into the pocket of his jacket, out of sight and out of reach.

'You can't do that!' she protested. 'That's my property!'

The look he turned on her said that he could do whatever he wanted and she couldn't stop him.

'I prefer to have your communication with the outside world under my control.'

'But how can I keep in touch with my mother—with home?'

A touch of panic made her voice raw. How would her mother cope if she wasn't at the end of a line to offer help if she was needed? The rough and ready support system she had been able to set in place might be enough, but only if Sarah could contact her daughter at any moment she felt she needed to.

'You will be able to phone Thorn Trees once a day to see how things are. But other than that—'

'It isn't enough!'

'It will have to be enough. Because that is how it is going to be.'

'But my mother—is unwell.'

She was severely tempted to move forward, try to snatch the phone from the pocket of his immaculately tailored jacket, but the urgent sense of need warred uncomfortably with a strong sense of self preservation. She was here, on her own, in his plane, thousands of feet up in the air. If she caused a scene, started a struggle, then she was at a disadvantage from the off. Nikos would only have to raise his voice and call his staff…

No, don't be ridiculous. He wouldn't even need to call

anyone, she acknowledged to herself. Nikos could see off her feeble attempt at resistance so easily that she would be a fool even to try it. But even so she still couldn't give in to such domineering behaviour.

'You have no right—!'

'I have every right. I am the one who makes the rules, not you. You are here because I allow you to be here—no other reason. And you are here to do a job.'

'A job I can't do without a phone…'

Her eyes went to the laptop case still in his possession, carefully tucked under his arm, and a shiver of cold panic ran along every nerve. Did he really mean to isolate her totally, have her under his complete control?

'Or my computer.'

'Any information or help you need will be provided once we are in my villa. All you have to do is ask.'

'I can't work that way.'

'You work any way that I ask of you.'

It was a deliberate verbal slap down, reminding her harshly just who was in charge here. And she would be every sort of a fool to forget that, Sadie reminded herself miserably. She had been in grave danger of forgetting just how important this job was to her.

She was grateful for the lifeline he had tossed her, the chance to let her mother stay in the only place where she felt safe. And now here she was, risking everything by setting herself against the only man who could ensure that would still happen. She should be thanking him, agreeing to go along with anything he suggested. But still—stealing her phone…!

'I do not want the paparazzi finding out anything about this,' Nikos went on, snatching the conversational rug from under her feet and stunning her into silence in the space of a single heartbeat.

That she understood. She had no argument against it, and she couldn't even try to find one. The paparazzi and the popular press had been the bane of their lives when she and Nikos had been together. They had plagued them incessantly, day in and day out. They had never had a moment's peace or time to themselves. She had hated it, been made miserable by the constant hounding, the pushing and shoving, the shouted demands and the incessant flashing of a hundred or more cameras.

And at the end… Sadie shivered at just the memory. At the end the relentless attentions of those snoopers had made everything a thousand times worse.

She understood why Nikos couldn't let his new fiancée go through that. But she wouldn't be human if she didn't feel a pang of jealousy at the protective way he was determined to shield her.

'You can trust me!'

The look he turned on her told her that he felt the opposite was true.

'Trust…' he said, drawing out the word until it was a sound of pure doubt, cynical and rough. 'Ah, yes, we had such a trusting relationship, didn't we?'

Sadie winced away from the contemptuous mockery of his tone. She had trusted him with her heart, her future, her life. And he had torn it all to pieces and tossed it back in her face.

'This isn't about you and me. And I wouldn't—'

'I trust no one.' It was a flat, cold statement. No room for negotiation. 'I find it's better that way. Now, if you will fasten your safety belt…'

'What a terribly sad way to live your life,' Sadie flung at him, but she knew that she had no option but to do as he said. The seat belt light was still flashing and the jet was already beginning to alter its path to turn in the circle needed for descent. Personal safety, if nothing else, demanded that she acted sensibly.

'That is my phone,' she managed, determined to keep the defiance up as she sank back into the soft leather of her seat and reached for the belt. 'And, paparazzi or not, you have no right…'

Except the right of possession, she acknowledged to herself as Nikos blatantly ignored her, strapping himself in. And in this case possession was all, because she had no hope that he would return the phone to her, no matter how she pleaded.

Miserably she yanked the seatbelt tight, tighter than it needed to be. And she forced herself to stare out of the window, blinking fiercely until the tears that burned at the back of her eyes ebbed away, leaving them dry and unfocussed. She wished she could do the same with her thoughts, driving away the bitter sting of the slap of reality right in her face.

Because nothing could bring home to her more definitely or more cruelly the way that, in Nikos's mind, she was now no longer part of his life than the nasty little exchange she had just endured. Nothing could make it plainer that she was firmly on the outside, kept from the centre of his world by high, strong fences, the 'Keep Out' signs clearly and forcefully displayed. He didn't even trust her, putting her so far outside any circle that could be termed his friends that she could only assume her place was amongst those he considered his enemies. And the thought of being considered an enemy by him made a sensation like the crawl of something cold and slimy slither down her spine.

Out beyond the window she could see the land below becoming clearer and clearer as the plane continued its descent. Down there was Greece, Venizelos Airport and the city of Athens itself. The last time she had been here it had been as the newly engaged fiancée of Nikos Konstantos. She had stared out of the window with keen interest, bubbling with excitement at the thought that she was going to set foot in the homeland of the man she loved for the very first time. How different was this arrival, with no sense of excitement or joy, only a terrible feeling of oppression and apprehension, uncertainty about what was to come.

Then she had felt as if she was coming home. As if she was launching a new beginning, one that would put the tensions and stresses that had ruined her family life behind her and put her on the path to a much happier future.

This time she had no idea what to expect. The prospect of what was ahead of her made her insides twist into tight knots of panic at the realisation that this time she was truly alone, without a single ally on her side. No one she could turn to for help or support.

She might understand, rationally at least, just why Nikos had felt that he needed to take her phone and her laptop. But that didn't stop the nasty, creeping sense of fear that there might be more to it than he was letting on.

Just what did he have planned for her? And why did she have the terrible feeling that in coming to Greece like this she had made the terrible mistake of jumping right out of the frying pan and into the fiercely blazing heart of a savagely burning fire?

CHAPTER SIX

MAY WAS SUPPOSED to be the best possible time to visit Greece. A time when the sun shone but the weather had yet to heat up to the baking temperatures of summer. Sadie had experienced some of that heat when she had visited Greece before and she had found it hard to cope. But then they had only stayed a couple of nights in the capital before flying to the tiny island of Icaros that had been owned by Nikos's family for generations going way, way back. Once there, she'd found the breezes from the sea had helped to ease the scorching temperatures and made life more enjoyable.

But Icaros was no longer owned by the Konstantos family. Sadie's father had seen to that. And the memory of just what Edwin had done was a troublesome worry, like the ache of a sore tooth, nagging at her mind all the time.

'How are you this morning?'

Nikos's voice startled her from her thoughts, making her jump nervously as he strolled out of the living room on to the wide main balcony where she had been trying to at least make a pretence of eating some of the breakfast that had been laid out on a table in the sunshine.

'I trust you spent a comfortable night?'

'That depends on what you mean by comfortable.'

Dressed more casually in the warmth of his native country, he was devastatingly dark and stunning in a soft white shirt and loose beige trousers. His feet were bare, lean and bronzed on the white stone of the balcony, so that he moved as silently and easily as some loose-limbed cat, every bit as lethally elegant and striking.

'The room was not to your satisfaction?'

Nikos strolled over to the table and picked up a bunch of grapes, plucking one from the stalk and tossing it into his mouth.

'My room was fine. As you know it had to be. This is a beautiful house.'

And if she needed anything to bring home to her just how far the Konstantos family had come since their lowest point five years before then this was it.

The villa had been a real surprise. The first of many. The first time Nikos had brought her to Athens they had stayed in his large apartment in the Kolonaki district, overlooking the Parthenon. That apartment had been impressive enough, but it was nothing when compared to the Villa Agnanti, where they had arrived late yesterday afternoon. Built into the side of a hill, the huge white house was on several levels, each one going lower down the cliff from the main road. From the lowest level you could walk out through the back gate, step out on to Schinias beach, where the crystal clear Aegean Sea lapped against the shore just metres away. Every single one of the bedrooms had a balcony that overlooked the ocean, but even the gentle sigh of the waves against the sand had not been soothing enough to ease Sadie into sleep last night. Instead she had lain awake and restless, wondering just what she had got herself into and how she was going to manage to handle things here.

'It has everything I need,' Nikos responded, but the flat, un-emotional level of his voice somehow communicated far more than what he actually said. It was what he had not said that seemed to reverberate underneath the words and gave them a very different emphasis from the one he had used.

'But you must know that I wouldn't be able to rest properly without knowing what was going on at home.'

Sadie adjusted her position against the balustrade, turning so that she was resting her back against the white stonework and looking straight into Nikos's dark, sculpted face, feeling the warmth of the morning sun beat down on the back of her head.

'You phoned Thorn Trees just before dinner. All was well then.'

'But I only had five minutes.'

Five minutes during which the door to the room she had been in was left open and she had been painfully aware of the way that Nikos was waiting for her beyond that door, no doubt listening to every word she said. She had felt like a prisoner under careful observation, unable to manage more than a few stilted sentences in response to her mother's unrestrained delight at knowing that she was safe in Thorn Trees for the time being at least.

Not that Sarah fully understood that their reprieve was only temporary. The joy that had rung in her mother's voice had been another twist of the knife in Sadie's already worried and aching heart. Her mother might think that Nikos had been wildly generous and unbelievably forgiving, she might believe that the stay of execution was permanent and for all time, but Sadie knew it was just that—a stay. And the way Nikos had behaved on the flight here, the fact that her phone and her laptop, her only means of communication with the outside world, were still firmly in his possession left her in no doubt that he wasn't planning on being forgiving or even kind, but on holding her ruthlessly to their bargain for as long as it took. And then…

And then?

The truth was that she had no idea at all what would happen next. When her time in Greece was up, when she had fulfilled her contract and Nikos and his fiancée were married, then what would happen?

Was the reprieve that he had granted them only for the length of time that she was working for him? And when that was done would he let them stay in Thorn Trees? She couldn't see it happening.

'Long enough to assure yourself that your mother is well. You are here to work.'

'Then let me get some work done! There's no way I can do anything without my laptop. And without meeting your bride.'

That came out more pointedly than she had planned. The truth was that just the thought of him marrying someone else twisted up her feelings so badly that she didn't know what to think or how to feel.

'My bride will not be here for some time. You will not be able to talk to her.'

'But that's ridiculous! How can I work on your—? We—'

To Sadie's horror her mixed up feelings seemed to have tangled on her tongue, making her stumble over the word.

'Your wedding—when I don't know who she is or what she likes? I need to talk to her.'

'You will talk to me.'

Nikos tossed another grape into his mouth and chewed on it before swallowing it down. Sadie found that the simple movement held her gaze transfixed on the lean line of his throat, the muscles moving under the smooth olive skin. She felt her own mouth dry in response, her own throat move as she swallowed too.

'I will tell you everything you need to know.'

'You will?'

Was that embarrassing croak really her voice? Sadie moved to the table set out on the balcony and reached for a glass of orange juice, gulping it down to ease the tight constriction of her throat.

'A wedding is a woman's most special day. She would want it to be absolutely perfect.'

'And it will be,' Nikos returned with smooth arrogance, clamping sharp white teeth down on another beautifully fresh grape. A tiny trickle of juice slid out on to his lips and he swept it away with a slick of his tongue.

Sadie forced her eyes down to study the surface of her drink as if it held the answer to some vitally important question. Anything to distract herself from the way that her thoughts were heading. Deep inside she was having to struggle with the wild, crazy impulse to move forward, press her mouth to that one small spot on his lips, to savour the sweetness of the grape combined with the intensely personal taste of Nikos's lips.

She was still fighting the sensual need, her fingers gripping her glass tightly, when Nikos spoke again.

'I will see to that.'

In the face of his cold confidence the rush of physical response faded as rapidly as it had come, leaving her feeling shivery and unsure, as if in the grip of a sudden fever. For a moment she had let herself forget how icily controlling and ruthless Nikos could be. And forgetting that was not a good idea.

'And you think that everything you do is so perfect? That you can never make a mistake?'

'Not perfect, no.'

Nikos pulled out one of the chairs and lowered himself into it, stretching out long legs in front of him, crossing them at the ankle. The change of position should have made him look more relaxed, at ease, but strangely it had exactly the opposite effect. He looked like nothing so much as a hunting tiger, lazily settling down to keep a watch on its prey before it decided whether it was worth the effort to pounce or not. The glass in her hand shook with the tremor of her grip and she hastily banged it down on the table, so as to avoid spilling some of the juice on to the stones of the balcony.

'And as to making mistakes, well, if I was immune to them then I would never have had anything to do with you.'

'But you can't take control of someone else's life like this. I would never let you get away with it... What?' she questioned in surprise as Nikos's low laughter broke into her outburst.

'I am only too well aware of that, *agapiti mou.*' The cynical emphasis on that *my dear* turned it into the exact opposite of any term of affection and the gleam in the golden eyes as he laughed up at her was totally lacking in any sort of warmth. 'Why do you think that I would prefer I kept you to myself while we work on plans for the wedding?'

'If you intend to go ahead and marry this girl this time.'

No sooner had the words escaped her than she wished them back. Too sharp, too bitter, they revealed far more of her personal thoughts than she had ever wanted. The last thing she wanted was for Nikos to feel there was any lingering bitterness about the fact that their marriage had never taken place. She was free of that—wasn't she?

'Do you doubt it?'

'What do you think? I have personal experience of just how much you mean your marriage proposals, remember?'

Nikos's mouth twisted slightly, his penetrating stare seeming to burn right into her soul.

'But I always intended to go ahead and marry you.'

'You did?'

Nikos swallowed some of his coffee, then grimaced in distaste.

'This stuff is cold. But no matter.' Pushing back his chair, he got to his feet again. 'We should be heading out anyway.'

'Heading out? Why? Where are we going?'

'You said that you wanted to know more about the wedding. What better way to start than with the place I have in mind for the ceremony? Go and collect whatever you will need. We leave in ten minutes.'

It was going to be a long day, Nikos reflected as he watched Sadie's retreating back, the sensual sway of her hips, as she made her way into the house. The morning sun beat down on his head and down below, at the bottom of the cliffs, the roar of the surf pounding against the shore was a constant background sound to everything.

A sound that fitted the restless hammering of his thoughts as he fought a constant battle to keep his more primitive male impulses under control. He was beginning to wonder just how long he could keep up this pretence of wanting to work with her on the wedding. The truth was that work had nothing at all to do with what he wanted to do with Sadie Carteret.

When he had walked out on to the balcony and seen her standing there, it had been all that he could do not to march across and grab her, pulling her hard against him and bringing his mouth down roughly on top of hers, kissing her until they were both reeling with hunger, their thoughts obliterated in the need that he knew would flare between them.

The sun had gleamed on the dark gloss of her hair, gilding the pale shoulders in the sleeveless red sundress. A red sundress that had big black buttons all the way from the dipping neckline right to where the hem swirled around her slender shapely calves. Those buttons had put the devil's torment into his mind, tempting him almost beyond endurance with images of closing his fingers over each one, sliding it carefully, slowly from its fastening, and then moving down. Exposing first the soft creamy curves of her breasts, the shadowed valley between them. A valley that he knew from experience—all too short an experience—would be warm and slightly moist, the intimate scent of her skin heightened by the heat of her body, reaching out to him and then falling away with each hasty, unevenly snatched breath she took.

And then moving lower, down to her waist, letting the folds of the soft material part over her hips, where the shadow of her sex showed beneath the delicate covering of her underwear. Lower still, until it fell away from her body, leaving her exposed and revealed to the hunger of his eyes, the touch of his hands.

No! With a rough jerk of his head, he pulled his mind away from the sensual thoughts that plagued him and forced them back on to the here and now.

Because here and now he had to concentrate on other things. But it was damn near impossible to concentrate on anything when all he wanted to do was to take Sadie to bed and spend the rest of the day sating himself in the soft warmth of her body.

She would let him too. Or at least she wouldn't put up much of a fight. He had seen it in her eyes when they had been on the balcony. The sensual awareness that she hadn't been able to hide. The way her head had gone back, her lips parting slightly, softly. The way that the dark pupils of her eyes had enlarged until her eyes were almost all black, only the faintest trace of mossy green at their edges.

If he had walked across to her then, taken the glass from her hand and replaced it against her lips with his own mouth, then she would not have protested. Or not much.

It would be that moment in his office all over again. The response that neither of them could hide. That he was damn sure he didn't want to hide. And that he knew Sadie was fighting to conceal from him now because she believed he was going to marry someone else.

A faint smile crossed his mouth as he followed Sadie inside. He was enjoying watching her struggle with the flames that flared between them and the feeling that she could not, must not act on them. He would keep her on that particular rack for a while longer. The end result, when he finally let her off, would be well worth waiting for.

'We're here.'

Sadie had to struggle to bite back the exclamation of relief when Nikos made his announcement perhaps fifty minutes later. Helicopter flights were not her favourite form of travel, and from the moment Nikos had led her from the house to his private helipad, where a gleaming machine that looked like nothing so much as a giant black dragonfly had waited for them, her stomach had been twisting tight with tension. And that sensation had been made all the worse by the way the limited space inside had forced her into close confinement with Nikos for the length of the flight.

He'd piloted the helicopter himself, and every movement of his tanned, muscular arms, the strength of his long fingers on the controls, had her mouth drying in sensual response, her own hands tightening on each other where they lay in her lap. So it was with a sense of escape that she watched the land, the first they had seen for the last twenty minutes of a journey which had been mostly over sparkling blue sea, come closer and closer as the helicopter descended.

'Where are we?' she asked when at last they were on the ground, with the engine turned off, and she was able to look around.

But Nikos was already out of the craft and, ducking to avoid the slowing blades, coming round to open the door on her side. It was as she set foot on the ground, the blast of heat hitting her after the controlled temperature inside the plane,

that recognition hit, and with it a cruel wave of desperate
memory. She knew this rugged shoreline, the steep cliffs that
rose above the sea. And there in the distance was the low,
white-painted, unexpectedly simple house where she had once
spent a magical couple of days when Nikos had first brought
her to Greece and to his family home.

'This is Icaros!'

She knew she looked as startled as she sounded, her head
coming up sharply in surprise, green eyes locking with cool
gold. And it was then that she realised he had been aiming for
just this response.

'You got the island back?'

Nikos's response was a curt nod.

'I got the island back,' he confirmed.

'Oh, I'm so glad about that.'

That made his eyes narrow in frank disbelief.

'You are?'

'Of course! I know how much this island means to your
family.'

It was in the tiny chapel here that his father and mother,
his grandparents and every great-grandparent they could remember had been married. A tradition that was vital to the
man Nikos was. And his sister, who had died as a baby, was
buried in the chapel grounds.

'So did your father.'

Nikos's tone was so savage that Sadie actually flinched
away from it, recoiling in her chair as if from a blow to her face.

'That was why he sold it to someone else instead of keeping it for himself. An extra fortune for him, and more of a
problem for me to get it back if I ever tried it. I would have
to negotiate with someone else and he thought he would be
able to watch.'

Sadie shivered both at that icy tone and at the thought of

how her father had behaved. The island had been one of the weapons Edwin had used against her when she had refused to believe that Nikos didn't really love her. If it was a love-match, her father had said, wouldn't she be marrying in the little island chapel, like every other Konstantos bride before her? And faced with that and so much other evidence, she had had no choice but to believe him.

She hadn't wanted to think that her father was right. Hadn't wanted to accept his bitter, cynical way of thinking about everything. He had been so totally obsessed with getting revenge on the Konstantos family that it had taken over his life. But she had no idea why.

'Do you know what started this crazy feud in the first place?' she asked impulsively, not caring if the question was wise or if it would push her even further into trouble with Nikos, raking up old bitter memories that were far better left buried.

'There was always rivalry between the families—in business dealings. But then it became personal, when the woman my grandfather was supposed to marry ran off with your grandfather instead. *Pappous* never forgot—or forgave. And he made sure that the Carterets paid for it financially. After that, if one family could attack the other in any way, they did.'

Nikos moved away from the helicopter and paced over to the edge of the cliff to stand staring out at the sea. His long body was silhouetted dark against the sunlight, the width of his shoulders seeming even more impressive than ever.

Suddenly, painfully, Sadie was reminded of the days when they had been together. When, if she had seen him like this, she would have been able to go up to him, slide her arms around that narrow waist until they met over the flat stomach. She could have rested her head against the powerful back, felt the heat of his skin through his shirt and inhaled the rich, intimate scent of his body.

That was how she had always dealt with difficult times in the past. Whatever mood he had been in, she had always been able to bring him round that way, to make him relax and smile again. More often than not he would turn in her arms, gathering her close to kiss her fiercely, until her head was spinning with happiness and desire.

That was how they had ended up in bed together the first time on that weekend before her wedding…

No, no, no!

Desperately she dragged her thoughts back from the painful path they were following. She must not let herself remember how it had once been. It was too cruel, too distressing. And all those 'once had beens' had never really existed. She had been living in a dream world, swallowing every deliberate lie that Nikos tossed her way and believing she had found the love of her life. The risks of even allowing such memories back into her life was too great to contemplate with any degree of safety. If she let them back into her mind, into her heart, then she would never be able to cope.

'There was more to it than that.' She tried to continue the conversation in order to distract herself from the torment of her memories. 'Something more recent that had made things even worse. My father was…*obsessed* is the only word. He'd always perpetuated the feud in a business sense, but something new happened to drive him even further into the depths of hatred for the Konstantos family. Into a determination to ruin them once and for all.'

'And you didn't know what that was?'

'No,' Sadie managed, her eyes now fixed on the horizon. Her heart was thudding erratically, making it difficult to breathe. She was too much on edge, too aware of the difference between being here now like this and the way things had been that first time to manage to control her voice.

'But I do know, in the end, it never truly brought him any real satisfaction. He drove his family and friends away because nothing else mattered to him. And he broke my mother's heart. I found out later that my mother had had an affair. It destroyed their marriage, but I'm sure it was because she felt neglected, abandoned because he was so obsessed.'

It was so much easier to talk like this when Nikos had his back to her. When she couldn't see his dark, stunning face and the cold contempt that burned in his eyes, thinned his beautiful, sensual mouth. Like this she could still pretend that they had some sort of a civilised relationship.

'We could—we could end it,' she suggested, buoyed up on a sudden rush of hope. 'We could say it stops right here and now and—'

'And what?' Nikos enquired, turning suddenly to face her again. 'And what, Sadie, *agapiti mou?* Hmm? We end it now and—what? Become close friends?'

He didn't have to explain how he felt about that. It was there in the disgust stamped clearly onto the beautifully carved features, in the twist to his lips, the bite of the words he flung into her face.

'No—not friends. We could never be that…'

'Not friends,' Nikos repeated with a brutal emphasis, his tongue curling in distaste on the word. 'Because friends would never turn friends out of their home. Because friends would waive the cost of the rent—or even the purchase price of a very expensive house.'

'No!' Sadie shook her head violently so that her dark hair spun out wildly in the sunshine. 'No—nothing like that!'

Did he really think that that was why she had proposed ending the feud? So that as her 'friend' he would feel obliged to let her off her debts and hand Thorn Trees over to her at a peppercorn rent? In the back of her mind she could hear once more that mocking 'mate's rates' that he had tossed at her in his office a couple of days before.

'You're right! We could never be friends. And I wouldn't want to be. All I meant was that we could call a halt to these stupid hostilities and—and live totally separate lives. There's no way we ever have to even see each other again.'

The thought seemed to stop her breath in her throat. She'd managed to get on with her life these past years by refusing to let herself even think about Nikos and pushing away every memory when it tried to surface. It had nearly broken her but she had managed it. Now it would all be to do again. And, knowing how hard it had been the first time, she flinched away from the prospect of going through it once more.

'And the sooner that happens, the better as far as I'm concerned.'

He was supposed to respond to that. She even paused, waiting for him to say something but Nikos remained strangely silent. Silent and still. Only the burn of his eyes, fixed on her, unblinking, seemed alive in his set and rigid face.

She should take that as a yes, Sadie decided. It certainly wasn't any sort of a no. Nothing like a rush to say that, no, they must not separate, must not be apart again. Of course not. But she wished he would say something. Anything.

And suddenly she had to speak again, if only to break the disturbing, nerve-stretching silence that had been going on for far too long.

'We'd better get this job done so that I can get out of here and be on my way.'

She would be professional if it killed her, she told herself. It was the only way she was going to get through this. She would do the best damn job she could, never put a foot wrong, and then Nikos would have no reason at all to find fault. No reason to go back on his word to let her mother stay in Thorn Trees.

But it was one thing to make that sort of a resolve, quite another to stick to it when every place they walked held a memory of the time when they had been together. Every path, every cove, even every rock, spoke of a happier time, a time when she had known the joy of love, even though it had all been a bitter deception and not the delight she had thought it to be.

It was almost as if Nikos knew what was in her thoughts, what had been in her heart when she had visited Icaros with him all those years before, and was now using it to torment her with the fact that this was where he would be marrying his new fiancée, the woman he loved. And it was when they crossed the little wooden bridge that led from the main island to the high headland, where the tiny chapel stood, that she knew she couldn't hold back any more. Coming to an abrupt halt, she turned to Nikos, brushing back the dark silk of the her hair that the winds had whipped into wild disorder around her face.

'Just why am I here?' she demanded, not caring if the words were wise.

Had she gone completely mad? the look he turned on her said. Did he have to explain everything to her? In words of one syllable?

'You are a wedding planner. I need to plan a wedding.'

The exaggerated clarity with which he spoke, a deliberate slowing down of his words, grated on her already overwrought nerves. He sounded as if he was having to explain to someone simple. Someone who would have difficulty in understanding what he said.

'But you could have anyone you wanted. There must be much more established—more successful—fashionable—wedding planners you could hire.'

'But I want you.'

What was it in his voice that made a shiver run over her skin, lifting the tiny hairs in a rush of apprehension? Sadie couldn't define it, and she wasn't sure that she really wanted to dig too deep and find out more than she wanted to know.

'Why me? Why none of the others?'

Nikos pushed open the door of the little chapel, the wood making a harsh scraping sound over the stone-flagged floor.

'You owe me,' he declared harshly. 'They don't.' And then, with an abrupt turn onto another conversational path that threw her completely off balance, he continued, 'Now, come inside and see the chapel.'

She didn't want to see the chapel, felt that it would destroy her totally to do so. It would take what was left of her shattered heart and grind it in the dust beneath Nikos's soft handmade boots. If the rest of the island had bitter memories for her, then the inside of the chapel belonged purely to Nikos and the woman he now planned to marry. He had never brought her in here when they had visited Icaros in the past. In fact, the tiny building had stayed securely locked and shuttered, and she had never even set foot on the worn wooden bridge that led to it. Further evidence, her father had said, of the way Nikos had never planned to make her his wife.

But when it came down to it, what choice did she have? She was here to do a job, as Nikos had just reminded her so brutally. And on that job depended her mother's peace of mind—possibly even her sanity, with the resulting repercussions for her small brother's happiness. She couldn't let them down. And so she drew in a deep, hopefully strengthening breath, squared her shoulders and made herself step over the threshold into the cool, shadowed interior of the little church.

After the brightness of the sunlight outside, it was all so dark and dim that she was almost blinded, barely able to see a metre or two ahead of her down the single narrow aisle between the rows of rough wooden pews. Nikos himself, standing before the simple altar, was once more just a silhouette, a solid more substantial shape in the hazy light that came through the narrow windows.

Perhaps it was because of the blackness, because she couldn't see his face or read his expression clearly. Perhaps it was that she had no choice but to accept that in planning to marry someone else Nikos had demonstrated so clearly that he had moved on from the bitter past they had once shared. But suddenly Sadie was hearing again her own voice inside her head.

We could end it, she had said, referring to the terrible feud between their families. The feud that had taken away too much and given nothing. *We could say it stops right here and now…*

If only they could. If only she and Nikos could find a way to start again, so that each of them could go on and live their lives without the terrible black shadow hanging over them. But how could she begin? If she could just get Nikos to trust her, even in the tiniest degree, then that would be a start.

A sudden rush of new-found determination pushed her up the aisle towards the still, silent figure standing by the altar steps. Face unreadable, arms folded across the width of his chest, Nikos watched her come.

'If you really want to employ me as your wedding planner then you have to let me do my job properly,' Sadie managed once she had drawn level with him, the words spluttering from her in a rush to get them out. 'You really don't need to keep my phone and my laptop under lock and key—I'm not going to sell your story.'

The cold-eyed look he turned on her told her that there was no way he believed her declaration.

'You did damn nearly everything else in the past,' Nikos flung at her. 'So you'll have to forgive me if I'm in no rush to believe you can be trusted now. We do this my way or not at all. And if you can't agree then you'll be on the first plane out of here….'

And if she was on the first plane out of Athens, then what would happen to her mother and George? Nikos had said that he would not take revenge on a child, but if she did not fulfil her part of the contract then what was to stop him going back on the deal and throwing her mother and brother out of the only home where they felt safe? Her insides knotted in raw panic at the thought.

She had promised her mother that she would keep her safe in her home for as long as she possibly could, and she would keep that promise if it killed her, she told herself. The one thing she had going for her in this situation was the fact that Nikos was getting married and, for reasons known best to himself, he wanted her to plan the event for him.

She was just going to have to ignore the fact that even thinking about it brought with it a sensation like a cruel knife being scraped over raw, sensitive skin. That the concern that Nikos showed for preserving his fiancée's anonymity, his involvement in this early stage of things, rubbed her face right in the difference between this wedding and the one he had been planning with her.

Had *appeared* to be planning with her, she corrected painfully.

She needed to put all those difficult feelings out of her mind. She had to refuse to let herself remember that she was trapped here, isolated with the man who had ruined her life and her family's. A man who now seemed hell-bent on using the hold he had over her to his own advantage, and taking a cruel and sadistic pleasure in doing just that.

Somehow she was going to have to pretend to herself that Nikos was just a client. Sighing inwardly, Sadie faced the impossibility of that task. Nikos could never be 'just' anything. But that was her only way through this situation. The only way she could handle this. Because she did have to handle this.

The truth was that Nikos held all the cards and he could

play them as he chose. The only single option left to her was to do the best job she could—and hope that Nikos had some sort of kind cell in his body that would push him to help her when she was done.

Otherwise she would be right back where she had started—or worse. And all of this would have been for nothing.

CHAPTER SEVEN

'YOU WILL WANT to phone your mother.'

After a journey back to the villa that had been completed in almost total silence, Nikos's first words on their arrival caught Sadie distinctly off balance, so that for a moment or two she could only stare at him in confusion, not quite sure she had heard him right.

'Did you not tell me that you needed to check on your mother and brother?'

'Oh, yes—but…' But she hadn't expected him to remember or, if he did, that he would be the one to prompt her into action rather than the other way about. After everything he'd said, she had never thought that he would be so generous— or so trusting.

'You can use the phone in my office—it's just through here.'

He led the way into a room at the back of the villa. One that had disturbing echoes of the office at the Konstantos building in which she had faced him—was it really only a couple of days before? Memories of that encounter threatened to drain the strength from her legs as she followed him, putting a fine tremor into the hand she held out for the phone he snatched up and passed to her.

'If you need the code for England then this is it…'

Nikos scrawled a number on a piece of paper and pushed it towards her. Then he pulled out a chair at the head of the desk and dropped down into it, switching on the computer before him as he did so.

Not quite so generous or so trusting after all, Sadie acknowledged privately to herself. He might have handed her the phone, but he was still staying around in the office to make sure that she didn't say anything he objected to. She was not to have any privacy with her phone call.

But she wasn't going to look any gift horses in the mouth. Her mother's mental balance and her own peace of mind were too important for that. So she pulled the sheet of paper towards her, punched in the numbers and pressed 'Dial'. Perching on the edge of the desk, with her back to Nikos, she waited anxiously for her mother to answer. She would know how things were from the moment that happened.

'H-Hello?'

Oh, no! Sadie closed her eyes briefly in distress, her shoulders tightening as tension held them taut. She knew that tone of voice and it meant there was a problem. Her mother was clearly in a very different frame of mind from the previous night.

'Mum, it's me—Sadie. How's things?'

'Sadie—where have you been all day. I've been expecting you to call…'

'I had things I had to do, Mum.'

Sadie kept her voice low, hunched herself over the phone, as if by doing so she could cut herself off from the man at the other side of the desk, where she hoped that the click of keyboard keys meant Nikos was concentrating on what he was doing and so wouldn't catch anything of her mother's words.

'I'm here to do a job, remember?'

'I know you said that—but do you have to be away so long?'

Sadie's heart sank at the querulous note in her mother's

voice, the way it rose so sharply on the final words. She was very much afraid that, without her there to supervise, Sarah hadn't taken her medication and so was worryingly off balance.

'It's only a couple of days.'

But that was longer than her mother had been left alone at any time since George's birth, she acknowledged. And clearly the older woman was finding it hard to cope.

'What is it, Mum? What's wrong?'

And suddenly it was as if her question had pressed a switch, making the words flow. Sadie could almost see her mother perched on the edge of her chair, her fine-boned face drawn taut with nervous tension as she gave voice to her fears. She couldn't believe that the letter Nikos had sent yesterday was real. It seemed impossible that it was true. Impossible that they wouldn't be forced out of their home after all.

'It will be fine, Mum.' She could only pray that she sounded convincing. That there was enough conviction in her words to get through the panicked haze inside her mother's head and reassure her. 'I promise you that everything's going to be fine.'

If she could believe that herself then everything would be so much easier.

'But how do you know that, Sadie? How can you be sure? How do you know that Nikos Konstantos will keep his word? What if he changes his mind?'

'That isn't going to happen. I won't let it happen, Mum. I've made sure of that.'

What else could she say? she asked herself. When she was so far away from home, how else could she persuade Sarah to calm down? And it seemed to have worked. The nervous questions eased, and she could hear her mother's breathing settle from the frantic, uneven gasps that had so worried her.

'I've got everything in hand,' she said again. 'You know you can rely on me.'

'You're sure? We can stay?'

'Mmm…'

The non-committal sound was all Sadie could manage. Painfully aware of Nikos's dark, silent presence behind her, she didn't dare to try for more. And even more than before she prayed that nothing her mother had said could reach him.

When she had explained the situation to Sarah on that first evening after her meeting with Nikos at Cambrelli's, she had deliberately aimed to emphasise the positive. Nikos was letting them stay in the house for now. And at least as long as Sadie was working for him they were safe. That was what she had to hold on to until she had any sort of a chance to think of any other way out of their situation. But she knew that by highlighting the good things she was risking letting her mother think that all was completely well and their future in Thorn Trees was assured.

But she hadn't dared risk anything else.

If Nikos had caught her mother's words then what was he going to think? Would he believe that she had taken too much for granted? That she had assumed he would hand over a house worth millions simply because she was doing a job for him, planning his wedding? A sneaking cold shiver ran down her spine at the thought of his possible reaction.

'Promise me.'

'I promise, Mum.'

And now at last it seemed that Sarah was convinced enough to let her go. Reluctantly, Sadie managed to say goodbye, switching off the phone as she fought to get her own disturbed and shaken mood back under control.

'Is something wrong?'

Nikos had caught her sigh, and it made her stomach lurch in apprehension at the thought that he might also have heard her mother's unwary comments after all.

'No—nothing. Everything's—fine.'

Her voice caught on that word, but she pulled herself together and returned the phone to its stand on the desk. The movement brought her close to an array of family photographs nearby. Some of them looked familiar, but she couldn't quite place why.

'Who's that?' She waved her hand in the direction of one particular frame.

It was a question she was obviously not supposed to ask, judging by the dark frown that Nikos turned in her direction.

'My father.'

'Really?'

Sadie's eyes went back to the man in the picture. A man who looked so very different from the one time she had met Nikos's father—thinner and older, and with his black hair almost totally grey—that she shook her head in confusion.

'He's changed a lot.'

'He's been ill.'

Nikos clearly had no intention of explaining further, and Sadie was about to give up on the photos when something about another picture tugged on her attention again.

'And the one behind it…?'

'My uncle Georgiou. He died five years ago.'

And that was all he was going to tell her.

'So—do you have any questions about the wedding—other than who exactly the members of my family are?' he prompted harshly, cutting across her hasty, uncomfortable apology in a way that made it plain that she had been slapped down, verbally at least.

She was to keep her mind on her job and nothing else. Besides, if Nikos's uncle had died so long ago then she had obviously never met him.

'Well, yes, lots—starting with the obvious. You know it's

ridiculous to expect me to work on this without any idea about your—your bride. I understand your need for privacy—but surely just a few basic facts…?'

She pulled a notepad towards her, picked up a pen.

'Like her age, colouring, name.'

'Why the hell do you do this?' Nikos said, so suddenly and unexpectedly that the pen that was resting on the notepad jerked sharply in her hand, shooting up across the page and etching a wild straight line into the paper.

Hastily she recovered herself.

'What?'

Did she know what it did to him, Nikos wondered, when she looked at him like that, with her eyes wide and shocked, blinking in confusion? Very possibly she did, and that was exactly why she reacted in that way—wide-eyed and innocent, like a startled deer.

'Why do I do what?'

'Why does a woman who walked out on her own wedding spend her time planning other people's big days?'

'Because I believe in marriage.'

She was definitely on edge as a result of his question, tension showing in her shoulders and the elegant line of her beautiful neck. It was just a damn torment that the way she held her head, the rapid rise and fall of her breathing, brought those creamy breasts into his line of vision, creating a devastating temptation with every breath she took.

'Marriage?' he scorned. 'Do you really? Why would you of all people think that marriage is important? Ah—but of course…'

He snapped his fingers, as if he had really just come to the realisation but the way that Sadie's eyes flared in response made it clear that she knew only too well the way his thoughts were heading.

'Marriage as a dynastic arrangement. Preferably with plenty of money as a sweetener and perhaps a lot of hot sex in order to avoid any boredom.'

'It's nothing of the sort!'

She was getting to her feet again, her eyes flashing fury, cheeks pink with indignation. The way her breathing had accelerated meant that her chest rose and fell rapidly and unevenly, pushing her breasts against the v-neck of her red dress with every movement. The heated clutch of lust low down in his body in response was hard and immediate, making him draw in his breath in a sharp, uncontrollable response.

'I also happen to believe in love—I do!' Sadie flung at him, when the effort to drag his gaze away from the creamy swell that rose and fell so distractingly made him glance at her with what she obviously saw as disbelief in his eyes.

And he didn't believe her. Why should he believe her? How could he believe someone who had manipulated and schemed so that her own wedding was just a distraction of his own attention that her father needed to complete his plan for the destruction of the Konstantos family? A plan that had very nearly achieved more destruction than it had ever aimed for when his father had tried to take his own life.

And Sadie had played her part in that too.

'Love!' Nikos scorned. 'What do you know about love? Have you ever felt real love for anyone—anyone but yourself?'

'Of course I have! You know I have! I—'

'Oh, don't try to tell me that I know you've loved because of the way you were with me!'

Unable to believe how outrageously she was still prepared to lie, Nikos flung the words at her in a black fury.

'*Thee mou,* don't you dare claim that you loved—even still love—me!'

Sadie's head snapped back, eyes closing briefly as if he had actually slapped her in the face. But she recovered quickly enough and turned on him instead.

'No, I'm not claiming that! I don't love you. If you want the truth…'

'Oh, by all means, let us have the truth,' Nikos drawled, when an unexpected catch in her breath had her stumbling over her next words. 'It is time there was a little honesty in this relationship.'

'Honesty?' Sadie echoed, injecting the word with so much cynicism that she almost felt it sharp as a razor on her tongue, ready to cut her to ribbons. 'If you want honesty, then I'll give you *honesty.*'

Once more she had to pause, to draw in a needed calming breath, and Nikos watched her with burning eyes, no trace of emotion on the stone wall of his face. And the need to drive something past that armoured wall drove her to lose control completely.

'The honest truth is that I don't love you. Of course I don't. The only feeling I have for you is loathing. I *hate* you. I would never have come to you, never have sought you out unless you were my very last chance. The only hope I had.'

The way his eyes narrowed, black brows snapping together in a dark frown made Sadie's stomach clench in sharp unease. Had she taken several steps too far, saying that? Given him too much ammunition to use against her if he wanted to? But then there was no way he couldn't know that she'd had to be desperate, on her very last chance, to be prepared to come to him, practically begging for a way to stay in Thorn Trees. He could never have doubted how worried she had to have been to turn to him. Nikos, of all people, would know that if she had had any other possible alternative then she would have used it if she could.

And it had felt so good to actually spit the words out and toss them in his face. To say the things that she had wanted to say five years before and never had the chance. When Nikos had come to the house that one last time, and her father had opened the door to him, she had been upstairs with her mother. Sarah had been pregnant with George and had been in such a state that there'd been no way Sadie could have left her, not even to face the man who had broken her heart and destroyed her life. So she had tossed down the stairs the lines that her father had given her to use and at the time had been thankful that that was all she'd had to do. That she hadn't had to actually confront Nikos about the things he had done. Because that would have been more than she could bear.

But this time it felt good to actually have the words on her tongue and to give them free range. So good that for a crazy, wild moment she didn't stop to think of what she was doing or of how dangerous it might be to let rip.

'And the only reason I'm here is because you asked me to do a job—to plan and organise your damn wedding! We had an agreement on that.'

'We did.'

Nikos's tone was surprisingly mild, but the burn of his eyes seemed to flay away a couple of precious layers of her skin, leaving her raw and hurting without even trying.

'And I will stick to that agreement, no matter how I feel about you personally. I'll give you every last bit of my expertise. I'll do the best job I can. Because that's what I promised.'

She had no other choice. If she didn't fulfil her side of the bargain, then what was to stop Nikos from reverting to the 'no way, no chance…go home and pack' stance that he had taken with her at first. Before his unexpected and almost unbelievable change of heart.

'But I'll not do it for you. I'm doing it for your bride, so that she can have a wonderful day even if—even if she is marrying you. And in order to do that...'

What had changed in his face, altered his expression? Some shift in his muscles or a different light in those searing eyes. Something very subtle but definitely there. And it changed everything in the space of a single heartbeat, disturbing the atmosphere so that she felt herself floundering, suddenly gasping for air as if she had gone down under water and her lungs were filling up with liquid.

'In order to do that?' he prompted smoothly as she fought to find her voice again.

'In order to do that I will need to meet her—talk with her.'

'No way.'

Leaning back in his chair, Nikos laced his hands behind his head, lifting his legs so that they rested on the polished wood surface, feet crossed at the ankles.

'But that's ridiculous. Impossible!'

His one-sided shrug dismissed her protest as totally irrelevant.

'That's how it's going to be.'

'But there's no way I can do my job if you won't tell me anything, not even her name.'

But once again they had reached a sticking point. She could see it in his eyes, in the set of his stubborn jaw. She had had all the factual information he was going to allow her.

But there was one more thing he wanted to tell her.

'All you need to know is that she is the only woman I have ever wanted to marry.'

Nikos was still lounging back in his chair, feet still on the desk. He looked supremely at ease, totally relaxed. But there was nothing comfortable or casual about the way that he added that final comment. Instead, he slipped it into her hard-won composure like the sharpest stiletto blade, sliding in between two of her ribs, aiming straight for her heart.

And it hurt so much that it destroyed every last trace of the already precarious self-control that she had been fighting to maintain ever since this conversation had started.

'I can't do this!' she declared, shaking her head in despair at the situation in which she found herself. 'I really can't! You have to see that. Here I am, trying to arrange a wedding for a bride who to all intents and purposes doesn't seem to exist.'

A stunning thought hit her, and she turned to glare into Nikos's watchful face, green eyes clashing with gold in deliberate challenge.

'She does exist, doesn't she?' He couldn't have brought her here on some sort of wild goose chase, could he? And if he had, then why?

Nikos adjusted his position, taking his hands from behind his head and raking both of them through his hair, ruffling its sleek darkness in a way that was dangerously appealing. Sadie's hands itched with the recollection of how it had felt to have the freedom to smooth through the black silky strands, curling them round her fingers.

'Oh, she exists,' he assured her. 'She's very definitely real.'

'Then I want you to get in touch with her.'

Reaching for the phone, she snatched it up and held it out to him.

'Get her on the phone—talk to her. You don't even have to let me speak to her. I'll just ask you the questions I need and you can get me her answers. At least that way I'll know she's been consulted—go on!' she insisted, when Nikos simply stayed where he was, watching her without moving.

But now the relaxed sprawl of his long body had changed, much as his expression had changed only moments before. There was a new tension in the muscular limbs, a tautness like that of a wary hunting animal, waiting and watching before it pounced upon its prey.

Furiously, she waved the telephone receiver in his face, not caring that the wildness of the gesture gave away far too much of the turmoil raging inside her.

'Talk to her!'

Another of those long silences, then at last Nikos shook his head, slowly and adamantly.

'No,' was all he said, making her stare at him in stupefied bewilderment.

'What do you mean, no?'

'I mean, I cannot call my prospective bride on the phone.'

'Why not? Where is she?'

'Right here.'

'What?'

The answer was so totally unexpected that Sadie actually jumped, looking round in shock. She almost expected to see Nikos's fiancée standing right behind her.

'There's no one—just me.'

A terrible, unbelievable thought dawned on her as she spoke, and slowly she turned back to face Nikos again.

'There's no one else here,' she said again, but this time it was a challenge.

'Exactly.'

Nikos removed his feet from the desk, stretched lazily and stood up, every moment slow and leisurely.

'The woman I want is right here.'

'But your fiancée…'

'There is no fiancée.'

He couldn't have said… Sadie found it impossible to believe that she had heard right. Desperately she shook her head, trying to clear her muddled thoughts.

'You brought me here to plan your wedding,' she protested,

knowing she was grasping at straws. Nikos's blank, emotionless face told her that he was not going to help her out in any way. 'You told me you had a fiancée…'

'If you remember rightly, I never said anything of the sort,' Nikos put in, with the sort of cold reasonableness that made her head spin in disbelief. 'I said that I wanted you to come here to arrange a wedding. But I never said who I planned to marry. And I never said that there was any other woman involved.'

The room seemed to be swirling round Sadie, blurring dangerously, setting off a terrible nausea in her stomach that she could barely control. Fearfully, she pressed her hands to her head, fingers tight against her temples, feeling worryingly as if her head might actually explode.

'You can't mean— You don't…'

'I can and I do.'

Nikos prowled closer, silent, deadly… And Sadie could only watch transfixed as his hand came out and touched her cheek, cupping her jaw softly as he lifted her face so that their gazes locked and held.

'What you are saying,' he said quietly, even gently, 'or trying to say, is that you are here because the one woman I have ever planned on marrying is you.'

CHAPTER EIGHT

THE ONE WOMAN I have ever planned on marrying is you.

The words pounded against Sadie's skull, making sense in a literal way, and yet stopping short of any possible sort of reality.

The one woman I have ever planned on marrying is you.

How could Nikos say that when it was so blatantly obviously not true? He had never really meant to marry her in the past, so why should anything be different now?

'No.'

She shook her head violently, but that only seemed to make the spinning sensation so much worse. It didn't even free her head from Nikos's grasp. Instead it seemed to bring her into closer contact with the warmth and strength of that hand, those long, powerful fingers closing over her jaw, firmer but not harder, warm and strong and shocking sensual. Shockingly welcome.

In the middle of all the chaos of her thoughts, the only thing that she could grab hold of was the way she wanted that hand to be there. She wanted to turn her head, her cheek, into the warmth of his palm, and feel the heat of his skin, taste it against her mouth.

And that was the exact opposite of how she thought she should be feeling. The way that she wanted to be feeling. The way that, rationally, she felt it was safe to be feeling.

It wasn't safe, it wasn't wise, it wasn't even damn well rational. But rational was so far from the way she was feeling that she frankly didn't care.

She only knew that all the time they had been in this room, when he had been standing or sitting so far way from her, she had wanted, needed, to bridge the gap between them. Had longed to come close and feel the heat of skin against skin, the pressure of hard bone under cushioning flesh. But it was only now, when he had made the move, that she actually realised that was what she had been feeling.

'No…' she tried again, but her voice had no more strength than the first time she had tried the word, less if anything, so that it croaked and broke in the middle as she spoke. 'You can't mean that.'

'Can't mean what, *glikia mou?*' Nikos questioned softly, the words seeming to shiver over her skin.

You can't have brought me here to—to…'

That word wouldn't form, and she didn't know whether it was because she didn't dare to face it or because of the way his thumb began to move, stroking slowly, delicately, over the angled line of her cheekbone and down the line of her jaw. Her legs were trembling, turning to cotton wool beneath her, and she felt as if the heat from that one small touch was radiating through her body, firing her blood, melting her bones. With a raw, jolting effort, she wrenched her head up and away from it, green eyes blazing into cloudy gold.

'You brought me here under false pretences!' she accused him furiously. 'You conned me—you've *kidnapped* me!'

'Kidnapped?'

Those beautiful eyes were deliberately wide and deceptively clear, with the look of the devil's innocence.

'Kidnapped you, *agapiti mou?* So tell me—when did I

force you, drag you on to my plane? When did I hold you hostage—lock you in your room, imprison you in the house?'

Strolling across the room to the door, he flung it open, gestured to indicate that she should walk past him if she wanted, out of the room, out of the villa…

And she very nearly took the option he offered. It was only as she made a single step forward that the rush of realisation came. He hadn't forced her in any way except mentally. He had told her that if she came with him to Greece he would let her mother and little George stay in the house that meant so much to them.

'You may leave any time you want.'

'No, I can't—and you know it! You made sure of that from the start. But I also know that I can't go through with what you have planned. And I really don't think that you can, either.'

'Why not?'

His question was so impossibly pleasant-toned that it was obvious the smoothness of his voice was hiding the dark, dangerous bite of something else. Something that Sadie shrank away from and yet was irresistibly drawn towards like a needle drawn to the most powerful magnet. She couldn't take her eyes from the sexy mouth that spoke those words, couldn't pull away from the sensual aura of his long, lean body that seemed to reach out to enclose her, holding her fixed as if her feet were nailed to the floor.

'Because what you said just does not make sense. You can't possibly want to marry me.'

'I can if that's what it takes.'

That had her frowning her total lack of understanding.

'Takes to do what?'

'To deal with what is between us.'

'There's nothing between us! Nothing at all.'

'Oh, but there is.'

When had he moved again, coming even closer, those soft boots making no sound on the polished floor?

'No!'

Sadie's hands came up between them, trying to push him away. But Nikos simply smiled and curled his fingers around hers, twining them together, soft and warm.

'There's this…'

Sadie's breath hitched in her throat as he lifted her hands to his mouth and pressed kisses on to each finger in turn. Her heart thudded hard in response to each warm, soft pressure of his mouth and she slicked a soft tongue over her own lips, easing the sudden disturbing dryness there.

'And there's this…'

Still holding both of her hands enclosed in one of his, he lifted the other to her head, stroking it down softly over her hair until she arched her neck to press herself against the caress, practically purring like a contented cat.

'And this…'

With a gentle but powerful tug, he jerked her close, so that the softness of her breasts was crushed against the hard wall of his chest, her hips cradled against his pelvis. The heat of his body flooded hers, making every nerve tingle into life, the pressure and the closeness making it impossible to be un-aware of the swollen evidence of his arousal so close to where an answering need was already beginning to uncoil low in her body.

'Nikos…' she murmured, and her voice had changed, soft-ened, the dryness of her throat making it husky and raw.

'Yes, *glikia mou?*'

Nikos sounded much the same, his words almost seeming to fray at the edges in the soft roughness of his tone. And, hearing it, Sadie knew that she had used up her ability to speak, her voice totally deserting her as she shook her head slowly, uncertainly. Unable to meet the fierce burn of that golden gaze, she lowered her eyes to look away. But that only meant that she was now staring straight at where their hands were still linked between them, his strong and dark against the paler slenderness of her own.

For a moment she froze, aware of the man who held her with every cell of her body, of the heat and hardness of him that seemed to surround her totally. If she breathed she inhaled the warm musky scent of him. She could see nothing but him. The bulk of his body enclosed hers so that she couldn't look past him to any other part of the room. And even though he hadn't kissed her she almost felt that if she ran her tongue over her lips once more she would taste the essential flavour of him.

'Sadie?'

Nikos's voice was a warning and an invitation all rolled into one. The same warning, the same invitation that his body held for her. The warning said that if she backed away now then this chance would never come again. The invitation was to all she wanted and more.

Deep in a corner of her mind some tiny shred of common sense cried a warning. But Sadie crushed it down until it was buried completely. She had no intention of heeding it or going along with common sense. This was what she had wanted from that moment in Nikos's office, and again in the plane on the way to Athens.

Then, the kiss, the caresses had been forbidden to her, because she had believed that he had a fiancée. Now there was no one to come between them, nothing to stop her. And she didn't want to stop.

The invitation was what she wanted. And the invitation was what she was going to accept.

Slowly, she lifted her head. This time her eyes met his full on and she didn't blink or look away.

'All right,' she said softly, but clearly, angling her head even more so that her mouth was his for the taking. 'Let's deal with what there is between us.'

The words were barely out of her mouth before they were crushed back under the pressure of his lips. But where she was expecting hard force, powerful passion, what she actually felt was slow, sensual enticement. The taking of her mouth with knowing skill. The wicked exploration of every inch. The slide of his hot tongue along the division between top and bottom lip, into the crevice at the corner and then back again, probing softly but insistently until she had no option but to let her head fall back and open to him completely.

And as she did so everything took fire. The slow, seductive moments were gone and all was heat and hunger and blazing, stinging passion that had her whimpering underneath his kiss, writhing up against him. Her breasts were crushed against his chest, her hips against the heat of him, and she flung her arms up and around his neck, holding his proud head down and close to her to prolong the kiss.

A kiss that now was no longer slow and seductive but hot and hard and demanding. A demand that she met willingly, gave back willingly. She felt Nikos's heart kick against his ribcage, lurching into a heavy pounding that she heard echoed in her own bloodstream as the heat of hunger flooded through her. Her hands clutched in his hair, her body writing against his as she felt the burn of his fingers trailing over her naked shoulders, down the length of her spine. His palms clamped over the swell of her buttocks, drawing her closer than ever before.

'Nikos…'

This time his name was a whimper of need against his mouth. A sound of encouragement driving him on. And she heard him mutter something in raw thick Greek as he adjusted his position, made it possible for him to obey her needy urgings.

She was spun round, lifted from her feet. The next moment she found that she had been deposited on the polished surface of the desk, the skirts of her red dress pushed up around her waist, the smooth wood cool against her legs. Nikos took advantage of her change in position as, one hand supporting her back, the other worked fast and urgently to unfasten the black buttons that held the sides of the dress together. And all the time his mouth followed the path of his hand, imprinting burning kisses over her skin.

The red linen fell away, exposing the creamy slopes of her breasts in the soft blue bra. Nikos's breath hissed in sharply between his teeth and he lifted his head slightly, one long finger reaching out to trace the outline of the scalloped edge, making her shudder in agonised response.

'Nikos…' she said again on a sound of protest, of need, and the shivers came again, harder, fiercer, as he cupped one aching breast, slipping his thumb inside the lacy material, stroking over her breast, circling a tightening nipple until she cried out in shocked response.

That cry was captured in his mouth again, swallowed down as he pulled her closer once more, angling her halfway down to the desk, supported only by the strength of his arm at her back. The heat of the other hard palm burned against her sensitive flesh as he pushed the pale blue cup aside, wrenching the straps of the bra over her shoulder and partway down one arm, imprisoning it against her side.

But her other hand was free and could reach out to the buttons on his shirt, wrenching them open with rather less finesse than the way he had dealt with unfastening her dress. She heard the material of his shirt rip slightly, the clatter of a button landing on the table, but couldn't find it in herself to care.

All she wanted was the feel of his skin, hot and silky, hazed with body hair, underneath her questing fingertips. A gasping sigh escaped her as she clawed at his chest, fingernails scraping lightly over the tight buds of his male nipples. Her mouth curled into a knowing smile as she heard a muttered imprecation in his native language, felt his strong body jerk in uncontrolled response.

'Yes, *gineka mou*,' he told her roughly, the movement of his mouth tormenting that achingly aroused tip of the breast beneath his lips, the heat of his breath feathering delight over the sensitised bud, making her writhe in delicious torment on the desk.

She heard the clatter of something—perhaps the pencil pot—being knocked aside, the thud of something landing on the floor, and Nikos's dark laughter against her skin was just an intensification of all the sensations that assailed her already.

'You are my woman,' he repeated. 'Mine.'

'Yours.'

It was a whispered echo, one that was choked off on a note of abandoned ecstasy as that hot and hungry mouth found her pouting nipple, sucking it deep into its moist heat and swirling a tormenting tongue around its yearning peak.'

'Yours!'

She arched up towards him, needing to intensify the sensations, the pressure, and felt his teeth gently scrape the distended tip. For a moment she completely lost herself, almost swooning away in pleasure and only coming back to herself when another new and stunning sensation hit.

Those knowing fingers had reached the heart of her, stroking tormentingly along the fine stretch of fabric between her legs, making her gasp aloud, her one free hand clutching at the fine cotton of his shirt, holding him when she feared he might move away. But all he planned to do was hook his fingers in the sides of her knickers, tugging them down along her thighs to expose her to him more openly. At first it was easy, but when they caught and tangled just below her knees he swore roughly and gave up trying for any sort of finesse. A couple of hard tugs and they had ripped apart at the seams, tossed away in an impatient, careless movement.

His mouth was where his fingers had been, kissing a burning path through the dark curls clustered between her legs, the wicked torment of his tongue swirling over delicate, receptive tissue, making it unfurl and respond like a rosebud opening towards the sunlight.

But she had had enough of waiting, had enough of the sensual agony of anticipation, delicious though it was. Her hands were shaking as she fumbled with his belt, clumsy with need and a desperate urgency. She was making a total hash of things when he laid a restraining hand over hers, and his hot mouth kissed the moans from her lips.

She heard the rasp of a zip and knew a moment of agonising tension, her breath held in her lungs, before he came back to her again. Lifting her so that she was half on, half off the edge of the desk, he opened her legs wide, knees bent, feet braced against the polished wood and moved between them. His mouth took hers again, his tongue probing deep, in the same moment that he used his hands on her hips to lift her, move her, then draw her down on to his hard, heated length.

'Nikos!'

His name was a long drawn out sigh of pure satisfaction and delight, and for a moment she would have been content to stay like that, close to him, filled with him, abandoned to him. But Nikos was not prepared to stay or wait. Already he was moving, stroking deep inside her, in and then withdrawing almost to the end, before plunging in deeply over and over again. Her hands were around his neck, fingers digging into his shoulders, her mouth moving against his jaw, kissing, licking, nipping at the stubble-roughened skin, tasting the salt of his sweat against her tongue. After only a very few seconds she had lost herself, unable to do anything other than absorb herself into the moment, giving herself up purely to sensation. Mindlessly, blindly, she was moving with him, on him, feeling him inside her, taking her higher, higher, until he finally pushed her over the edge into the blazing, whirling oblivion of total ecstasy.

She heard a voice cry out aloud, and from a distance vaguely realised that it was her own, but she was too far gone to care if anyone had heard. A few seconds later she heard Nikos too give a raw, exultant sound as he followed her, and for a long time after that she knew nothing at all. Only the slow, slow drift back to a form of reality, a sort of return to consciousness, but one that kept floating to and fro, coming back to her and then swirling away again. Taking her into the glowing darkness where all she was aware of was the strength of Nikos's arms around her, the heave of his chest as he fought for control of his breathing, the thud of his heart underneath the powerful ribcage, the scent of his skin where her head rested, totally limp and spent against his shoulder.

It was a good thing there was the desk here to support them both, Nikos reflected, when some of the thundering haze had left his head and he could finally begin to think again. At least it was there to take some of Sadie's weight and allow him to prop himself up on it until he recovered. After the onslaught of wild and uncontrolled passion that had taken him—taken them both—by storm, he seemed to have lost the ability to focus, to recognise reality when it came back to him. He felt as if he had been at the centre of some furious whirlwind, snatched out of reality and spun around in a spiralling, blazing typhoon of feeling, then dumped back down on still not quite steady ground again, not knowing which was up and which was down. His arms were shaking, his legs unsteady beneath him, and he still couldn't manage to get enough air into his raw and aching lungs. He was quite sure that the racing of his heart would never ease so that his pulse rate could return to anything approaching normal.

And Sadie was in no better state than he was. In fact, she seemed barely conscious, her head dropped on to his shoulder, her breath scorching his skin as she too struggled to breathe normally. Her whole body sagged against him, limp as a marionette with its strings completely snapped in two, nothing to hold her upright. And the only noise in the room was the raw, unsteady sound of their breathing, that and the faint splash of the waves coming in to shore out beyond the open window, where ordinary everyday life was going on as normal, oblivious to the wild and sensual storm that had raged inside the villa.

But they could not stay shielded from reality for ever. Sooner or later life must start again. Someone might come in. They had to collect their thoughts and return to normality, for the time being at least.

And then they would have to face the repercussions of what had just happened here.

He for one would have to face the fact that he had stupidly, blindly, rashly rushed into this without a thought, without a moment's consideration for common sense or practicality. Or even, *Thee mou,* even safety.

He had just had sex with the woman he had hated for the past five years, a woman he had learned the hard way not to trust. And he had done it without even the use of a condom to protect him now and against the future. He hadn't paused to think about such things but had been totally at the mercy of his body, his libido, as lust-crazed as a newly horny teenager—and every bit as mindless. Both of them had been wildly out of control, responding in such a white hot fury of desire that any weak attempt at a rational thought had been burned away, reduced to ashes in the blazing conflagration they had lit between them.

And the worst, the most stupid thing of all was that he would do it again at the drop of a hat. Even now, with his breathing barely back under control, his pulse-rate still far from normal, she only had to move and he could inhale the clean, fresh scent of her skin, overlaid with some delicate flowery perfume, or feel the brush of her soft hair against his cheek and the heavy throb of blood would start to rise within his body. If she sighed, exhaling warm breath against his shoulder, so that it slid in to caress the skin at the open neck of his shirt, then he was still tempted to turn and take her in his arms once more, to kiss her hard and strong. Kiss her until their senses woke again, fought off the lassitude of satiation, destroyed all rational thought, and the heated hunger and yearning took possession of them once more.

She would go with him too. He knew that without thinking. Knew that he had only to touch her and both of them would go up in flames, the most basic, most primitive parts of their natures responding to the instinctive demands of their bodies.

And that would be the most damnably stupid way to behave imaginable.

He had to get a grip and fast, before things got completely out of control.

'Sadie…'

At first he found that his voice wouldn't work and he had to clear his throat and try again.

'Sadie.'

This time she heard and lifted her head, slowly and with difficulty. Her eyes, still hazed by the storm that had assailed her, the explosive climax that had erupted like a volcano in her slender form, blinked and tried to focus, almost but not quite succeeding.

'We need to talk—' Nikos began, then broke off as the sound of the phone ringing broke through the silence, tearing apart the atmosphere that was rich with the heavy clouds of sensuality and jolting them back to the real world in a second.

Automatically Nikos reached for it, lifted the receiver.

'Yes?'

Hearing his father's voice, he knew that he had no alternative but to deal with whatever Petros had on his mind.

'I have to take this,' he said to Sadie. 'And I may be some time.'

She looked as if she needed the time anyway. How could they talk when she was so clearly not yet capable of doing so? Besides, he would prefer to have some time to collect his thoughts himself. Decide just where he was going to go from here.

But first he had to deal with his father. And if Petros discovered who was with him—if Sadie spoke or gave herself away—then they would be back on the terrible old treadmill of the family feud before he could stop it. That had complicated his relationship with Sadie once before. He was not about to let it happen again.

'Go and clean yourself up…'

His eyes swept over her dishevelled state, the red linen dress hanging open heavily crumpled and creased, her bra half on and half off, and her knickers discarded in two separate tiny pieces on the office floor. Stooping, he picked them up and dropped them into her hand while she was still clearly gathering her thoughts.

'But…' she began, but Nikos shook his head, hunching one shoulder to hold the phone between it and his ear as he turned her and propelled her firmly towards the door.

'Take a shower—or maybe swim in the pool. I'll come and find you when I'm ready. What?'

The sound of his father's voice drew his attention back to the phone conversation.

'No,' he said, in response to the older man's enquiry as to whether the person he was with should take priority over him. 'No one important. Nothing that can't wait.'

It was only when the door slammed closed behind Sadie that he realised that he had spoken in English. Even when talking to his father.

CHAPTER NINE

WELL, THAT WAS her well and truly dismissed.

Finding herself in the corridor outside the study door without quite realising how she had got there, Sadie did not quite know whether to explode in fury or to burst into shocked, bewildered tears. She was quite capable of both, and the resulting combination was so volatile that any one tiny incident would be enough to spark it off.

For a moment she actually considered spinning round, marching back into the room and confronting Nikos over what he had said. Snatching the phone receiver from his hand and tossing it well out of reach if she had to. She even half turned, ready to do just that. But the thought of the danger she might put herself in—and her mother and George—as a result stayed her movement and kept her feet moving right in the direction that was safest: away from the office and back up to the safety of her bedroom, moving as quickly as she could for fear that she might meet some member of staff which, in her present dishevelled and disreputable state, would be just the worst thing possible.

It couldn't be more obvious just what she had been up to. Her crumpled dress was still gaping over her exposed breasts and her underwear barely existed. Looking down at the totally destroyed knickers she held in her hand, she couldn't suppress a shudder of revulsion at the sight of them and the thought of just how they had got into that appalling mess.

And she had only herself to blame.

'All right.' She could hear her own voice in her thoughts, husky and inviting—seductively so. 'Let's deal with what there is between us.'

And of course Nikos had taken her at her word. Who could blame him? She'd handed herself to him on a plate, without a care or thought for the consequences.

Reaching her bedroom, she hurried inside and slammed the door shut, leaning back against it as the last of her mental strength deserted her, leaving her shaking and distraught.

She hadn't even had the sense to insist that he use a condom! She had made every possible mistake in the book. The sort of thing that even her twenty-year-old self had managed to handle so much better in the past. So she had no right to complain if Nikos had treated her like the easy conquest he obviously believed her to be.

The easy conquest she had let herself be.

With a cry of disgust and horror, Sadie flung the ruined knickers into the wastepaper bin, not caring that one part of them fell far short, fluttering down on to the deep gold carpet like a wounded and dying bird. A moment later the dress and bra followed them, tossed aside in total revulsion. She couldn't wait to get out of them as soon as possible. Just the thought of ever wearing them again made her stomach heave.

Take a shower, Nikos had said. He was damn right. She would take a shower. She needed to wash the scent of him from her body, the taste of him from her mouth. If only she could erase her memories as easily, she told herself as she stood under a hot shower, letting the water pound down on her head, sluice over her skin. She scrubbed every inch of her body, shampooed her hair twice, but she still couldn't get rid of the feeling of having been used and then discarded without a second thought.

'Damn him!'

Finally having to get out of the shower, before she reduced her skin to the state of a prune, Sadie rubbed at her hair with a towel, ruffling it impossibly.

'Damn, damn, damn him!'

She was strongly tempted to put on fresh clothes, stamp back down to the study—but to do so would reveal to Nikos just how much his behaviour had upset her. That and the fact that as long as she didn't push things to the ultimate extreme then her mother and George were still safe in Thorn Trees. If she made one mistake, took a wrong step, then she had little doubt that Nikos would carry out his threat to have them thrown out of their home and on to the streets.

Or would he do that anyway? The frantic movements of Sadie's hands stopped and she stared at herself in the mirror, looking anxiously at her face where the flush of colour from the heat of the shower was now fading rapidly from her cheeks. Just what did Nikos plan to do next?

He had got her here under false pretences, claiming that he needed her to plan and organise his wedding. But there had been no wedding to organise at all. It had been nothing but a deceit from start to finish. So had this really been his plan? To get her back into his bed—not that she had actually been in his *bed*, she acknowledged grimly. She had fallen right into his hands like a ripe plum the first time he had kissed her in his London office and that must have given him the cue he had needed—if in fact he'd needed any such thing—to go ahead with the scheme that she now saw was his ultimate attack on her family and his personal revenge on her.

'But there must be some arrangement we can come to!

Surely there's something I can do—anything...' Her own words came back to haunt her, making hot colour flood every inch of her body. She could see just how that had sounded— and how Nikos would naturally have interpreted it.

'And exactly what sort of services did you have in mind?' he had come back at her. 'What exactly are you offering...?'

She'd denied it furiously at the time, but obviously she had put a seed in his mind and he had determined that the real price of letting her stay in Thorn Trees was to be paid in kind.

If she had any sense, she'd be out of here—fast. She had her passport. She might just be able to afford a plane ticket home on the little that was left on her credit card—she hoped.

If she had any sense, or any choice. Because she could be in no doubt as to what would happen if she did run out on Nikos now. Just the thought of her mother being thrown out of her home after the delight of thinking that she had been given a reprieve made the tears burn at the back of Sadie's eyes. She couldn't even call the police and tell them how Nikos had kidnapped her. As he had pointed out, he had used no sort of force, and she had come with him only too willingly.

And if they heard about what had just happened in Nikos's office...

She was trapped, but that didn't mean she had to sit back and take whatever Nikos tossed her way. A quick glance at the clock revealed how much time had gone by since he had bundled her—as 'no one important'—so unceremoniously out of his office. Any minute now, she was sure that he would be coming looking for her.

She didn't want him to come here and think that she had been sitting waiting for him. Sitting on the bed waiting for him. What she wanted him to think was that she didn't care. That the words he'd said had had no effect on her.

Take a shower he'd said—or have a swim.

She'd do that. Moving hastily to one of the drawers in the wardrobe, she pulled out the swimming costume she had tossed into her case at the very last minute, never really expecting that she would ever have a chance to wear it, and hurried herself into it. When Nikos came to find her, she wouldn't be here. She would be in the pool—swimming and relaxing in the sun, without a care in the world. And not sparing a single thought for the heated scene in the office.

It almost worked. The warmth of the sun beating down on her head, the cool clarity of the water, the regular physical activity of the strokes up and down the pool soothed her jangled nerves. She actually managed to empty her head of the anxious thoughts that preyed on her mind and focus only on what she was doing. Until the moment that a dark shape blotted out the sun and there was a splash, a brief glimpse of a powerful form slicing into the pool in a perfect dive. A few seconds later, Nikos surfaced, dashing water from his face, tossing back his wet hair as he trod water beside her.

'So this is where you've been hiding yourself.'

'Hardly hiding,' Sadie managed with careful insouciance. 'It's a hot day and I didn't want to waste the luxury of having a pool at my disposal.'

She prayed that he would take the ragged edge to her voice as being the result of the exertion of her swimming and not what it truly was—an uncontrollable response to his closeness. To the sight of the powerful chest and shoulders that showed above the surface of the water, black body hair slicked against the tanned skin under which the strong muscles flexed and bunched as he balanced carefully, keeping himself from going under.

'After all, it's not every day I see a pool like this. And I do love swimming.'

In spite of her effort to control it, a note of longing slid into her voice. For years now there had been no time for this sort of relaxation, not even in the local public pool. Her mother's illness and the need to look after George had taken up any free time she had from running the business.

'You should have stayed with me.'

Nikos pushed both hands through the darkness of his hair that lay sleek and black, plastered to the strong shape of his skull by the weight of the water. Drops of moisture still lay along the broad slash of his cheekbones, sparkling in the sunlight as he turned towards her.

'You should have stayed with me, *glikia mou,*' he returned sardonically. 'Then you could have swum in a pool like this every single day.'

'Not if I'd married you when it was originally planned— five years ago.'

The memory of the way that Nikos had trapped her, making her believe that he was going to marry someone else, made her voice sharp. No matter how much she tried to push it out of her mind that telling phrase, *'The one woman I have ever planned on marrying is you'* just would not be pushed away. She knew he didn't mean it—how could he mean it?—but still her brain just wouldn't let it go. And she was forced to face up to the appalling possibility that in a moment of weakness, of longing for it to be so, she had let that lying declaration influence her earlier, when he had kissed her.

Was it possible that she had actually let herself believe that he meant it? And that that was the reason—part of the reason—why she had given in so easily—too easily—to his passionate seduction?

'You weren't in such good financial shape then, were you? Or why else would you have come after me in the first place?'

One corner of Nikos's sensual mouth quirked up into a half

smile. Seeing it, Sadie couldn't help but remember the sexual devastation that mouth had worked on her hungry body when he had kissed every inch of her while she had lain, aroused and yearning, on the polished surface of his office desk. The heat that raced through her veins at the memory had no chance at all of being cooled by the lapping water of the pool.

'Didn't what happened earlier give you the answer to that?' he drawled softly, the wicked gleam in his eyes heightened by the glare of the sun. 'Surely that would have shown you that you have no need at all of false modesty?'

'There's nothing false about it,' Sadie flashed back. 'Or modest. I'm simply being realistic and honest—and I wish that you would do me the courtesy of being the same. The fact is that if I had not been Edwin Carteret's daughter and the heiress to his fortune then there is no way you would ever have sought me out at the start.'

'I—' Nikos began, but she had seen the look in his eyes, the subtle change in his expression, and knew that, in spite of the way that he tried to hide it, he was thinking through his response very carefully, planning exactly what to say.

'Honesty, Nikos. You owe me at least that.'

For a long moment his golden eyes locked with hers and she could almost hear his clever, ruthless brain working through the possibilities and coming to a decision.

'Honestly, then…' he said at last. 'The answer is no. If you had not been your father's daughter, then I would never have sought you out in the first place.'

If he had reached out and grabbed her hard by the shoulders, wrenching her towards him and pushing her down hard underneath the cool water, then he couldn't have caused more of a shock to her heart. *But, be honest with yourself too*, Sadie reproached her foolish mind. *Did you really think there would be any other answer*? Hoping for a different response was such a foolish weakness. A wishful fantasy that could never be achieved.

'And, yes, I lied to you—or at least kept from you the fact that the Konstantos finances were not in the best possible shape. But who can blame me when I already had overwhelming evidence of the way your father was working to bring the corporation down?'

'You could have confided in me. Trusted me.'

'Trust!' Nikos scorned, throwing back his dark head in a laugh that seemed to turn the air around them into ice and then splinter it into a million tiny pieces. 'You dare talk to me about trust when all the time you were part of the whole conspiracy your father had set up. When I was fighting for my life—for my family's life—you were there, just waiting to stab me in the back.'

That was more than Sadie could take. In the past she had been forced to play along with her father's wicked plans, forced to keep silent about everything that was going on in order to keep her mother and her as yet unborn baby brother safe. Now that part of the problem, at least, was all over. Her father was dead; he couldn't hurt anyone any more.

'If I hadn't done what I did, then you would have lost your fight.'

'What?'

Nikos's intent stare from swiftly narrowed eyes made her wish that she could duck down into the water to escape it. But she'd embarked on telling at least this part of the truth. She couldn't back down now. She doubted that Nikos would let her do it even if she tried.

'And just what is that supposed to mean?'

Dredging up her courage, Sadie faced him across the clear sparkling surface of the water. Pride stiffened her spine and brought her chin up defiantly.

'You talk about fighting for your family's life, but it was really just to preserve some part of the family fortune.'

She'd missed something there. The sudden hard blink of those amazing eyes told her that she wasn't actually in possession of all the facts. Once again Nikos had adjusted his expression, so that the one he showed to her was a carefully assumed mask, a polished veneer that hid reality behind it. But she couldn't stop to think about what it might mean. So far Nikos had seemed to hold the upper hand, but in this at least there was something he didn't know and she was determined to make sure he knew it.

'And if I hadn't done what I did then you would have lost everything. As it was, you were at least left with the Atlantis.'

As she named the one rather run-down hotel that was all her father had let Nikos and his family keep from their ruined estates, she knew that she had hit home. If her words had been a slap in his face, then he couldn't have reacted more strongly. His whole body stilled in the water, his face freezing into a hard, set façade that gave away nothing of what he was thinking.

'And what do you know about the Atlantis?'

But the sense of injustice that had buoyed her up until now had abruptly deserted Sadie, taking all her courage with it. She couldn't take any more, couldn't face that ruthlessly probing look, the way that his amazing eyes seemed to burn right into her.

'Enough,' was all she could manage, and at the sight of his frown, the way that his mouth opened to demand more of an answer, her nerve broke completely and she made a swift dive into the water, kicking out her legs and turning to swim away, heading for the far side of the pool as fast as she could.

But of course Nikos came after her, his stronger stroke and more powerful muscles driving him through the water so that he came up behind her fast, long arms reaching out to grab at her. He caught her just as she was about to scramble up the ladder on to the side, hauling her back against him and twisting her round in his arms so that she was forced to face him.

'Explain,' he snarled, issuing an order with no doubt at all that it would be obeyed.

But Sadie's throat seemed to have closed up over the words she needed and she couldn't get them out. She could only shake her head in despair, sending her soaking wet hair flying so that drops of water spun off and landed on Nikos's face, close to his eyes. He dashed them away with a brusque movement of his head, refusing to let go of her arms in order to brush them aside. Instead his grip around her arms tightened and he gave her a rough little shake, pushing her to give him the answer he wanted.

'Explain,' he said again, and to her astonishment just a little of the attacking quality had gone out of his voice. 'What you are saying doesn't make sense. When your father set out to bring down the Konstantos Corporation, he damn nearly succeeded. In fact, we thought that he had done just that—taken everything. It was only later—after...'

Again he made a slight adjustment, as if there was something he was covering up, hiding from her.

'Afterwards that I discovered Carteret had not quite managed to take everything. There was one little piece of the company left—something that had either been too small or, in his mind, not important enough to bother with...'

As he paused to stare into her eyes, Sadie found the strength to fill in the gap.

'The Atlantis.'

Nikos nodded sombrely, his eyes never leaving her face. But she felt the way his hard grip on her arms had eased and knew it meant his mood had changed.

'And you can only know about this because you were

somehow involved in making sure that it was still ours. That it was the one thing your father didn't get his hands on.'

It was a statement not a question. His tone of voice and the dark-eyed look was levelled on her face told her that he already knew the answer but he wanted her to confirm it.

'Yes.'

As she nodded her head in response, she suddenly felt a rush of pride and determination come back to bring new strength to her mind and body.

'Yes, I was involved. I could have saved the island for you—my father actually gave me the choice, and I considered it at first—but at the time I felt choosing the one small hotel that was the other thing he had been prepared to concede might actually be more practical help than the sentimental attachment you had to Icaros. And I was right, wasn't I?'

Nikos nodded slowly, his expression unreadable, bronze eyes clouded and hooded, hiding his real feelings from her.

'You were right.'

'Of course I was right—and bloody stupid at the same time. I knew you and so I chose the Atlantis, giving you at least a small business—something to keep you and the Konstantos Corporation one step away from complete bankruptcy. I chose that and I gave you a small start on the path to building your fortune back up again. Of course I didn't know how quickly and easily you would do it. Or how you would then use all that you'd gained—all the money, all the power—to turn the tables on me and my family. To have your revenge—'

'My revenge on your father,' Nikos put in, but she was too caught up in what she was saying, fighting too hard against the tide of pain and bitter memories that threatened to swamp her, to hear what he was saying or to understand the tone in which he'd said it.

'And then when you'd succeeded in getting back everything

you'd ever lost—and more—when you'd finished taking your revenge on my father—when he was dead and free from your cruel quest for vengeance—that was when Fate really dealt you an ace card. Because when you moved to take possession of Thorn Trees you just thought that you were going to throw us out. That you would kick us out of the family home and never see any of the damn Carterets any more. But of course I had to go and turn up in your office, begging for a chance to stay in the house—offering to do anything. And that…'

Her voice cracked on the words so that she had to struggle to go on.

'And that was when you decided you could have it all. The money, the businesses, the house—and the ultimate satisfaction: your final, personal revenge on me.'

Nikos's hands had fallen from her arms, setting her free, and so now, unable to bear the closeness to him any longer, she pulled away, swallowing hard to fight against the tears clogging her throat.

'Well, you got what you wanted, Nikos—every last little bit of it. Two days ago you said that you weren't satisfied—that the revenge you'd taken hadn't been enough. Well, I hope to hell you're satisfied now—you damn well ought to be, because to be honest there's nothing left for you to take!'

She had to get away. Had to. If she stayed any longer then she was going to give herself away completely. Eyes stinging, vision blurred, she somehow managed to find the ladder out of the pool and scrambled up it.

'No!'

But Nikos was only seconds behind her, vaulting out of the water and coming after her. He quickly caught up with her, grabbing her arm again to whirl her round to face him.

'No, you're wrong. Revenge doesn't come into it any more.'

'It doesn't?'

'No. It may have started that way but along the way things changed.'

'Changed how?'

Nikos's mouth twisted slightly, and just for a moment that clear golden gaze didn't quite meet hers.

'Along the way I abandoned revenge for something far more basic.'

Sadie frowned her confusion.

'Basic? So tell me what is more "basic" than revenge?'

Nikos didn't answer. But then he didn't have to. Looking into his eyes, Sadie saw just what he meant. It was written there, clear and plain to see.

What was a more basic drive than revenge? There was just one answer. Lust. Physical desire. Sexual passion. That was what had driven him from the start and what was still behind everything he did. An intense, searing physical need that obliterated everything else, burning it up in its heat. She recognised that, and understood it. Because didn't she feel the same whenever he touched her? Hadn't she just been so driven out of her mind with the same overwhelming hunger that she had let him take her on the desk in his office without a hint of a thought?

'So…' Her throat was painfully dry, cracking on the single word. 'So the whole story of a fiancée?'

'I told you. It was a pretence from start to finish. It had to be.'

Nikos dropped his head, resting his forehead on Sadie's so that his eyes burned into her from mere inches away.

'How could there be someone else when I never got you out of my head? You ruined me for any other woman. You got under my skin and I never got rid of you.'

'No—no one else?'

That was so much more than she had ever anticipated that her head swam under the impact of it.

'How could I kiss you like this…?'

His mouth took hers, slow and sensual, heating her blood in an instant and making her sway unsteadily on her feet.

'…if there was anyone else? How could I touch you…?'

If his kiss had been a sensual assault then his caress, the way his hands swept over her body, was like throwing a lighted match on to bone-dry tinder, making her skin flame in a second, setting her pulse racing between one uneven breath and another.

'And how could I ever think of taking another woman to my bed when the only one I ever wanted is right here…?'

The one woman I have ever planned on marrying is you.

The words that Nikos had spoken in his office came back to tempt and torment her. Tempting because she so wanted them to be true. Tormenting because she could scarcely begin to imagine that he could actually mean them.

And yet when she had insisted that he tell her about his imaginary fiancée—oh, dear heaven—he had also said: *She is the only woman I have ever wanted to marry.*

Was the world really spinning round her as she felt it was? Had she been out in the sun too long? Or was it really possible…? Could she believe a word he was saying?

But then Nikos took her lips again and she suddenly knew with a sense of total conviction that deep down she really didn't care. All she needed, all she ever wanted most in the world, was right here before her in the shape of this man. The man she had fallen for five years before. And she had never managed to recover from that infatuation ever since.

She was sinking deep into the spell of sensuality he was weaving, definitely going down for the third time. But at the same time a tiny, barely audible voice of instinct was whispering inside her head that there was something wrong, something missing, but she couldn't begin to think what. And quite frankly she didn't even want to try.

His hands were hot on her body, smoothing over the tingling flesh exposed by her plain black swimming costume. The stretchy material had almost totally dried in the sun, but the heat of the day was as nothing when compared with the flames that were flaring inside, burning her up with the yearning need that he could create so easily. One broad palm cupped her breast, the thumb stroking wickedly erotic circles over her nipple so that she shuddered in uncontrolled response, feeling that she might actually collapse into a molten pool right at his feet. Against her stomach she could feel the hard ridge of his erection, and moist heat flooded between her legs in response.

'So…'

Nervously, she slicked her tongue over her lips to moisten them enough to get the words she needed out of her mouth.

'So—when we first met—would you have married me?'

'Hell, yes. I'd have done anything to get you into my bed.'

That scorching, exciting mouth was doing amazing things to her. Tracing a burning path down her throat, over the exposed slope of her breast. When it caught one pouting nipple into its moist heat, suckling it through the black material of her costume, she cried aloud in response to the stinging pleasure-pain that sizzled through every nerve, destroying thought, leaving only space in her mind for the throbbing need she couldn't deny.

'Do you doubt it?' Nikos questioned against her skin, his breath on the question feathering over the moistened nipple, making it burn with even greater need.

'No…'

It was a moan of response and she shook her head vigorously, well past the point of being able to think about doubting anything. Her world was made up of just three things—herself, this man, and the wild sexual hunger that was blazing between them.

'Then come with me now—come back to my bed, *glikia mou,* and let me show you exactly what I mean.'

She meant to answer, Sadie told herself. She had to answer—because there was only one possible response she could give him. But she wasn't completely sure whether the wild, fervent *yes* that was burning in her thoughts had actually translated itself into sound or not.

But obviously it had—or it just didn't matter and the way that she returned his kiss gave Nikos the answer he'd been waiting for. Because he didn't ask any more questions or hesitate for a second. Instead he swung her up off her feet and into his arms and carried her out of the blazing sun into the coolness of the house and up the stairs, heading for his bedroom.

CHAPTER TEN

THE LATE MORNING sun coming through the window and onto her face finally dragged Sadie from the deep, exhausted sleep into which she had fallen well after midnight. Yawning and stretching, she felt the faint aches in her body after the night of passion she had shared with Nikos.

A long, long night of passion that had followed on from the equally ardent afternoon they had spent in bed too. At some point they had emerged to eat a meal, drink some wine, but the food had barely been touched before Nikos had leaned across the table, catching her chin in his hand and drawing her face towards him to plant another long, lingering kiss on her partly open mouth. Sadie had responded with equal enthusiasm, and soon they had abandoned all pretence of wanting to eat and headed back to the bedroom.

She could still feel the places where Nikos had kissed her, caressed her, finding pleasure spots she hadn't known existed, opening a world of sensual delights to her with every second that had passed. The scent of his body still permeated the sheets, and if she rolled over she could see the indentation on the pillows where his head had rested when they had finally succumbed to sleep.

And she could even still taste him on her mouth. If she

licked her lips then her tongue caught the faint flavour of Nikos's skin, the salty tang of his sweat, the deeply personal memory of his tongue tangling intimately with hers.

Sighing contentedly, she stretched again, savouring the memory that the taste brought back to her.

The taste of her first, her one and only lover.

The taste of the one man she had ever loved.

Her heart kicked hard and sharp at the thought, pushing her upright in the bed, staring sightlessly out of the window to where the clear blue Aegean Sea lapped lazily against the shoreline below.

The one man she had ever loved and the one man she still loved with all her heart.

She drew in a sharp, raw-edged breath at the realisation that this was how it was, and nothing she could do would ever change it. She had fallen head over heels in love with Nikos in the first moment she had met him and nothing had changed since. All that had happened, all that had come between them, had never managed to destroy the way she felt, even when she'd believed it had. Deep in her heart, the feelings had remained just the same. She still loved him; she would always love him.

And Nikos?

Now she realised just what she had been trying to grasp hold of in her mind yesterday by the pool, when Nikos's kisses and caresses had driven her so distracted with need that she hadn't been able to think of her own name, let alone grasp the elusive, whispering little voice that had tried to warn her that not all was well. That there was something she really should be thinking of before she jumped in too deep and let the dark waters of sexuality close right over her head.

Now, too late, she knew what it was—and she also knew that it meant that her life would never be the same. She also knew that it had been too late yesterday, too late from the moment she had confronted Nikos in his London office, seeing him again for the first time. Too late to go back to her old way of life, to managing to live without Nikos in it, without knowing that she still loved him. From the moment she had set eyes on him again she had fallen right back in love with him—though in those first days she had never realised the truth.

If, in fact, she had ever really fallen out of love with him. She had been terrified of being in love with a man who didn't love her at all. And so she had forced herself to believe that she hated him because it was safer for her, easier that way.

'Safer!'

Sadie actually spoken the word aloud, the way she was feeling turning it into a sound of shaken laughter. *Safer* just didn't come into it. *Safer* wasn't possible. Because the truth was that she had done exactly that, no matter how careful her personal safeguards had been.

She was in love with Nikos Konstantos and Nikos… Well, Nikos *wanted* her. He desired her intensely sexually; she could be in no doubt about that. He had spent last night and half of yesterday proving just that to her. He might even want to marry her. But only to get her into his bed and keep her there. He'd said as much yesterday.

'Hell, yes. I'd have done anything to get you into my bed.'

But he had spoken no word of love. Had never shown any sign of even considering that such an emotion existed. And probably, for Nikos, it never had. He had never loved her in the past, didn't love her now. And there was no hope that he would ever come to love her at any time in the future—if they had one together.

'Oh, Nikos!'

Sighing, Sadie forced herself to throw back the covers and get out of bed. What was it they said about the cold light of dawn? Yesterday had been wonderful, the night a sensual fantasy come true. But now, with the morning light shining bright on the new day, and with Nikos no longer in her bed to kiss her distracted, keep her thoughts from the 'what nexts' and 'if onlys' that plagued her, she was forced to face the probability that last night had not been a beginning, a start to a future, but instead a one-off final fling.

Wasn't it far more likely that Nikos had seen last night as a way, as he had said, 'to deal with what is between us'? To get her out of his system once and for all. He had made no promise, offered her nothing else. And she would be all kinds of a fool if she looked for anything.

But for now she'd take what was on offer, she resolved as she headed for the bathroom and the shower. The truth was that she was weak enough to admit to settling for anything. Just one more day…just one more time…

That phrase was still repeating inside her head when, fresh from her shower, naked and with dripping hair, she wandered back into the bedroom. Only to stop dead at the sight of the dark figure standing by the window.

'Nikos!'

With the sun blazing behind him, his imposing frame was just a black silhouette, his face a shadowed blank. But there was something about the way he stood, a tension in the broad shoulders under the soft blue linen shirt, in the way his hands were pushed deep into the pockets of his pale trousers, that warned her about his mood. He was not here for light conversation, and if she was any judge he was definitely not here to resume the lovemaking that had occupied so much of the night.

'What is it?' she asked sharply in the same moment that he spoke too.

'We need to talk.'

It clashed with her own words, but she caught it and it sent her spirits, already only precariously balanced between good and low, plummeting right down on to the floor beneath her bare feet. How many ominous, difficult conversations had begun with just those words? *We need to talk* implied that something had gone wrong—or was about to go wrong.

But what?

'OK.'

It was all she could manage, and in a way that was totally ridiculous after the night they had just spent together she found herself wishing that she had wrapped a towel around her before she had left the bathroom. Standing here like this, totally naked, she felt so vulnerable and exposed, needing to hide. She certainly didn't feel up to any 'we need to talk' type of discussion anyway.

'Not like this. Get some clothes on first.'

Obviously Nikos felt the same about her appearance. Which should have been a relief but, in fact, only added to her tension. Last night, nothing would have distracted him from the fact that she was naked—or from taking full advantage of it. Now it was an awkward obstacle in the way of what he wanted to get done.

Which didn't promise well for this talk.

'Of course.'

But her clothes were in her room, not here in Nikos's bedroom where they had spent the night.

'I'll…'

But Nikos was already moving, heading for the door as if he couldn't get out of there quickly enough.

'I'll be in my office,' he tossed over his shoulder at her.

'I'll be there.'

Somehow Sadie managed to keep her tone buoyant, when in fact, it should have been sinking with her spirits. She had admitted to herself that she expected her dismissal from his life to come sooner rather than later, but not this soon. She doubted if Nikos even heard her anyway, as the door swung to behind his hasty exit.

He was a fool, Nikos told himself as he headed for the stairs, the pace of his steps matching the state of his thoughts. A stupid, total fool and he had just proved it to himself.

He should have known. He did know, damn it! He'd left Sadie sleeping in his bed this morning and she had been totally naked then. And then, when he had gone into the room and heard the shower running in the bathroom, any idiot would have assumed that when she emerged she was not likely to be wearing any clothes.

But he had not been thinking straight. With his mind so full of the news he had been given this morning, he hadn't been thinking about anything else at all. And so when Sadie had finally emerged, beautifully naked, with her soft skin still pink and glowing from the shower, the sight had hit him like a blow to his already unfocussed head. And that was something he didn't need. In two ways.

He already had the image of Sadie's naked body in his mind. *Gamato,* after last night he knew that it was etched there permanently, never to be erased. If he had hoped that the sensory indulgence of the past eighteen hours or so would sate him on her charms and leave him free to live his life again, then he had been very badly mistaken. There was no way he was sated at all. The truth was that he doubted if he ever would be. There was no way he could have enough of Sadie Carteret, and one passionate night of total abandon had done nothing to appease the appetite he had for her.

If anything, it had only whetted it so that he was far hungrier now than he had ever been in the years they had been apart.

And that was why the article he had read in the English gossip columns had sent his mental temperature soaring, making any sort of rational thought impossible.

'Gamoto!'

It was also impossible to sit down and wait for Sadie to appear. The thought that he might have actually started to trust her when the truth was that he was being led around by his nose—or another part of his anatomy—twisted cruelly in his guts.

She was down quicker than he had anticipated. And where he had been sure that, realising something was up, she would dress carefully for maximum impact—something like the fantasy come true of that red dress came to mind—he found he couldn't have been more wrong.

Sadie had clearly rushed into her clothes, grabbing at the first thing that came to hand. And the first thing was a pair of worn denim jeans and a plain white v-necked tee shirt, her face clear of any make-up, pale against the still-damp darkness of her hair. Not that it helped any. The truth was that she was hellishly sexy in anything. And with the memory of her gloriously naked body in his arms, in his bed—underneath him, warm and willing all through the night and again in the bedroom just now—he had to make a fearsome effort to keep his eyes on her face. Because it was her face that he needed to see. He needed to look into her eyes, read her expression. That way he might have some chance of finding out what was going on in her conniving little mind.

'What is it?'

So she was going for wide-eyed innocence. With just a touch of defiance. It was the look she'd had on her face the last time he'd seen her five years before. He didn't want to look too closely at the memories that dredged up.

The newspaper was still lying on the desk, exactly as he had left it to go upstairs. He picked it up and tossed it towards her.

'Read that.'

He knew exactly the moment she registered what the photograph showed by the way that the colour shifted in her face and she bit down hard on her lower lip, white teeth digging into the soft pink. With an effort Nikos suppressed an urge to go to her and tell her to stop, to run his thumb over the damage she was inflicting on herself.

'Well?' he barked, when she had obviously taken in all she needed to, had dropped the paper back on to the desk and was preparing her answer.

'Well, what?'

What did he expect her to say? Sadie asked herself. And, perhaps more to the point, was there really any point in saying anything? From the thunderous dark frown on his face, he had clearly already tried her, acting as judge and jury, found her guilty and was now prepared to pronounce sentence.

'I don't know anything about this.'

A wave of her hand indicated the incriminating photograph. And she had to admit that she understood only too well just why he was so angry.

She had come downstairs, feeling shaken and on edge, apprehensive as to what was ahead of her. From the mood Nikos was in it was obvious that something had gone terribly wrong, though she had no idea what. The only thing that she could think of was that Nikos had had second thoughts about the passion they had shared in the night and was going to tell her it was all over. That had been bad enough. But this she was totally unprepared for.

'I *don't!*' she repeated when he turned a frankly sceptical look on her, making it plain that he had no intention of believing a word she said.

The picture was of the two of them in Cambrelli's just a few nights before. And it had been taken in the moment that she had leaned forward, stretched out a hand to touch him.

She hadn't actually made contact at the time, but from the angle the photograph had been taken it looked as if she had. And in the way their heads were inclined towards each other, eyes locked, seeing nothing else, no one else, the picture seemed to tell a story. A totally inaccurate story, but one that was encapsulated in the headline that ran along the top of the page.

'Together again!' it read, and the rest of the short article interpreted the scene in the way that she supposed it must have looked to an outsider. The sexy Greek billionaire and his marriage-shy ex-fiancée seemed to be back together, it claimed. They had met for a secret tryst in a down-market restaurant where they'd appeared to be getting closer by the second.

'Well, I don't see why you're so angry that we were seen together. I mean…'

Desperate to lighten the atmosphere, she tried a flippant shrug and knew immediately that she'd hit the wrong note.

'Look, it's not as if you really have a fiancée who would be worried or hurt by it.'

'Do you think that I give a damn about that?'

Sadie had no answer for him. Instead, she was busy trying to work out just what had happened.

'The storm…' she said slowly as realisation dawned. 'There was a storm that night, and what I thought was lightning…'

'Was in fact the paparazzo you had tipped off that we would be there.'

'What? No—of course not! How could you think that I would do that? Why would I do that?'

'Two words,' Nikos stated with deadly venom. 'Thorn Trees.'

'Th-Thorn Trees?'

Sadie frowned disbelievingly, rubbed hard at her temples where a headache was beginning to form. The abrupt transition from waking up happy and sensually contented to this fraught and tension-filled atmosphere was a terrible shock to her system. And now that Nikos seemed even more aggressive and antagonistic she was finding it even harder to think straight.

'I don't understand—why would this have anything to do with Thorn Trees?'

'Don't play games, *agapiti mou,*' Nikos scorned savagely. 'Do you think that I cannot add two and two together?'

'And come up with five, obviously!' Sadie flung back. 'Or more like five hundred. I don't see how you can make the connection, but I'm sure you're going to tell me.'

'Isn't it obvious?'

'Not to me. You're going to have to explain yourself.'

Nikos flung up his hands in an exaggerated expression of exasperation and his breath hissed in through his teeth in a sigh of dark irritation

'"I won't let it happen, Mum,"' he said suddenly. '"I've made sure of that. I've got everything in hand."'

For a second Sadie didn't realise what was happening, couldn't understand where the words had come from. But then she realised that he was quoting her own conversation with her mother on the phone the day before.

'I was talking about the wedding planning job I was doing—I thought I was doing—for you.'

Her legs felt distinctly unsteady beneath her so she pulled out the chair from the desk and rested her hands on the back of it, letting it support her as she faced him.

'I don't know what else you think I had planned.'

The furious glare Nikos shot her told her that he still believed she knew exactly what he was saying, but she refused to be intimidated by it, staring him out though it took all her courage to do so. Eventually he raked both hands through his hair again and muttered something dark and hostile in thickly accented Greek.

'The dinner at Cambrelli's was after you came to my office to ask—to beg—for a way of staying in Thorn Trees.'

'I know. And after you refused to help at all.'

'Exactly. In response to which you said that you would do anything—anything at all—if it meant you could stay in the house.'

The realisation of the truth hit her in the face like a slap, and she was so very grateful for the fact that she was supporting herself on the back of the chair as the shock of it made her head spin nauseously.

'You really believe that in order to get what I want I alerted the press to the fact that we were meeting—gave them a photo opportunity?'

The swift, sharp inclination of his dark head to one side was Nikos's silent acknowledgement that she was on the right track. But it still didn't make any sense that she could see.

'But I don't understand—why would that help me twist your arm over Thorn Trees?'

'Because we had been seen together. Because it was assumed—implied—that our relationship was back on.'

'But it isn't—wasn't…'

Which did she mean? Which was right? She really didn't know.

'We knew that. No one else. And not knowing that, how would it have looked if it became known that I had taken possession of Thorn Trees after all. That I had thrown my fiancée's mother and little brother out of their home? Perhaps out of spite for the fact that you had refused to get back with me again…'

'You think that I would have used this picture as some sort of moral blackmail—a bargaining tool to get what I wanted?'

'Why not? It is a technique worthy of your father at his best—or do I mean his worst? He would be proud of you, Sadie *mou*. You have clearly learned a great deal from him.'

'I've learned nothing!'

Raising her voice like this was probably a big mistake, but to be honest she didn't really care. She wanted to make her point as emphatically as she could.

'I've learned nothing from my father—and I wouldn't want to! The cold-blooded way he went about everything appalled me. I hated it. My father thought he could run people's lives—rather like you, in fact. It made my life a misery—my mother's too—and everyone else's around us!'

'And you expect me to believe that?'

'Do you know what?'

Sadie flung up her arms now, in a gesture that was very similar to the one that Nikos had used a few moments earlier—and expressing the same sort of exasperation.

'I don't really care! You're so obviously dead set against me—and so convinced that you're damn well right—it seems to me there's very little point in even trying to explain. I'm never going to persuade you of anything else. So I might as well just stop trying.'

And she'd have to admit that she lost Thorn Trees too, she acknowledged privately to herself. There was no way Nikos was going to let her stay in the house now, under any circumstances. She didn't dare to let herself consider that thought any further for fear that it would take all the strength from her. And she already felt as if she was fighting for her life.

'You're right,' Nikos conceded unexpectedly, shrugging his broad shoulders in a way that made her mouth drop open slightly in astonishment and disbelief. 'It really doesn't matter any more now. If anything, it makes things easier.'

And that was the last thing she had expected. So much so that she took a step back in shock, eyeing him warily, as if she believed that he might have changed shape and persona right in front of her, turning into some totally different, totally alien being right before her eyes.

'Easier in what way?'

He looked straight at her, those gleaming golden eyes locking with her confused green ones. And he actually smiled. But it wasn't a smile that warmed her in any way, or even lifted the atmosphere in the room. Instead it sent a cold, creeping sensation sliding down her spine in dread of what was coming next.

'When we marry, it won't be such a shock to the world—the gossip columns will already have had a field-day.'

Sadie shook her head in confusion. She couldn't have heard right.

'We aren't getting married.'

'Oh, but we are.'

Nikos put one hand down on the top of the desk, pressing hard on it as he leaned towards her.

'It's the obvious solution, isn't it?'

'Not to me. You haven't even asked me!'

'Do I need to ask?' he stunned her by saying. 'I told you—you are the only woman I've ever wanted to marry.'

And he truly thought that that made it all fine. The belief was stamped onto his dark features, drawing the muscles tight around his mouth.

'Yes, in order to have me in your bed!'

If she'd expected him to look mortified, even disconcerted, then she was very badly mistaken.

'And what better reason is there for being together?' he countered dismissively.

There's love, and caring for each other… But she didn't dare say it, couldn't even find the strength to open her mouth to speak the words. Obviously they had never crossed Nikos's mind, and were never likely to do so at any point in the future.

'We're great together sexually,' Nikos went on, confirming her fears. 'The best. You have to agree there. Last night proved that. I want more of that.'

'And me?' Sadie had to force the words from her tight and painful throat so they sounded raw and rusty, breaking apart at the edges. 'What do I get out of this?'

Again he looked stunned that she had to ask.

'Do I really have to tell you? You get to be my wife—to have all the wealth and luxury you could ever want. Everything you've ever dreamed of. I'll never look at another woman as long as we are together. And I'll give you Thorn Trees too—as a wedding gift. I'll sign it over to you on our wedding day.'

It was the fact that he thought it was enough that finished her. Nikos obviously felt he was offering her everything she wanted, so why was she even hesitating?

Because what he was offering was everything he thought she had ever dreamed of but nothing that she truly wanted.

She couldn't do it. It was her worst nightmare come true, possibly even worse than the last time he had wanted to marry her. Because at least then she had believed—had deceived herself—that he loved her. Now she no longer had even that comforting delusion.

'No.'

The stark rejection was all that she could manage. Besides, what else was there to say? There was no point in even trying to explain. The two of them were on opposite sides of a huge, gaping cavern, and there was no way at all of bridging the gap that yawned between them.

'Why not? After all, you were prepared to marry me for money once before. What's different now?'

If he had tossed a bucket of icy water right in her face then he couldn't have brought her to her senses any quicker. What was she doing even standing here like this, listening to him?

She had lost. That was the plain and simple fact. And the only thing she could hope for now was to get out of here with a shred of her dignity intact.

'What's different? Everything. Every damn thing. But I couldn't expect you to understand that.'

'Try me.'

Sadie had turned on her way towards the door, but those two words had her swinging back, looking him straight in the eye. If she had seen any sign there then, damn it, she might actually have tried. But Nikos's gaze was pure golden ice, no trace of emotion, no flicker of doubt to give her hope that they were even speaking the same language.

'You can't even see that it's the fact you have to ask that is the problem. If you think any woman would accept a proposal like that then you have to be out of your mind.'

Then, knowing that she had well and truly burned her boats, that she had to get out of here before she collapsed completely, she forced herself to continue her walk to the door, not daring to spare him even the briefest of glances.

'I'm going to my room to pack—and then I'm leaving—getting out of here. But don't worry. I don't expect you to get out the executive jet just for me. If you can order me a taxi to the airport, then I'll take it from there.'

CHAPTER ELEVEN

HE LET HER GO.

Nikos made no response to her outburst, and he didn't even attempt to come after her, to try to stop her. He just stayed exactly where he was and watched in total silence as she walked away from him, down the corridor and up the stairs. And for that Sadie could only be intensely grateful.

If he had made one move to stop her or even said a single thing then she knew that she would have fallen apart, gone to pieces in the space between one heartbeat and another. But when he said nothing and simply let her go she managed to get to the top of the stairs before the tears that had been pushing at the back of her eyes spilled out on to her cheeks, and she had to pause for a moment to draw in a shaky breath, fight with herself for control.

He hadn't even thought her worth fighting for. She had turned down his proposal of marriage—such as it was—and that was that. There was nothing more to do or say. She had said that she was leaving and that was the only alternative left open to her. She didn't dare to think of what would happen when she got home and told her mother that they had to move out. But she would face that when the time came. For now, she had to pack.

It didn't take long. She hadn't brought very much with her, and she certainly wasn't going to stay around to make sure everything was put neatly in the case. As long as she emptied the room and got out of here, that was all that mattered. She didn't even expect to see Nikos again.

So it was a shock to her when, after a brief knock, the door swung open and Nikos came into the room. Sadie's heart jolted against her ribs at the sight of him. Just for a moment she couldn't stop herself from wondering...

But, no, of course he hadn't come upstairs to try and per-suade her not to leave, or even to talk to her. Instead, his face more shuttered and closed off than ever before, his eyes hooded, he waved a hand towards the case that she had just fastened where it lay on the bed.

'This ready?'

'Yes.'

'Then I'll take it down for you.'

So he had come to help her on her way. To make sure that she left the villa as speedily as possible. At least she didn't feel she had to thank him for his consideration.

Instead she grabbed her handbag and jacket and followed Nikos down the stairs to the hall. No taxi, Sadie noted. Obviously it hadn't yet arrived. She just wished it would hurry up and get here. Every moment that she had to stay seemed to be dragged out beyond endurance, stretching her strength to its limits.

'You'll need these.'

Nikos was holding something out to her. Her laptop and her mobile phone. It was as she took the latter, preparing to drop it into her bag, that realisation dawned with a kick of shock.

'My mother!'

In the heady intoxication of the previous afternoon and night, the shock to the system that this morning had become, she had forgotten to phone and check how her mother was.

And now, checking her phone, she saw that she had forgotten to charge it up too. The battery was completely dead.

'Use the phone in the office.'

Nikos's voice make her start, glancing up at him with wide startled eyes.

'Are you sure?'

'Of course I'm sure. Do you think that the price of a phone call bothers me?'

The office was just as they had left it, the newspaper still lying opened on the surface of the desk. But somehow it was the other, earlier time they had been in there that now burned in Sadie's mind. She couldn't push from her thoughts the memory of how she had been half on and half off that polished surface, her clothes wildly disordered and her senses spinning off into ecstasies as she clung to Nikos's powerful form, her mouth melded to his.

Feeling the fiery colour rush up into her cheeks at just the thought, she grabbed at the phone in a fury of embarrassment. But just as she did so Nikos's hand came down on top of hers, making her start as the heat of his skin burned into hers.

'One thing,' he said abruptly, his voice harsh. 'This feud stops now. Here. It's over.'

'Do you think that I would say something to my mother that would incite that appalling hatred all over again? I just want to put it all behind me.'

She knew that the way she snatched her hand out from under his looked antagonistic, even hostile, but she felt as if her fingers might actually be scorched by the touch of his, so that she would branded for life if she didn't pull away.

Luckily Sarah was back on good form again, so the phone call to her mother took only minutes. Feeling both relieved and ill at ease, Sadie carefully replaced the receiver, glancing at the clock as she did so.

'What time is the taxi coming?'

'It isn't,' Nikos stunned her by saying. 'At least not yet. We still need to talk.'

'Didn't you say everything? No?'

She was stunned to see him shake his dark head. But then she thought she saw where he was going with this. The conversation she had just had with her mother.

'I know I didn't tell her—and I'm sorry. I couldn't do it like that, over the phone. But I promise you'll get the house back. We'll be out of there before you blink. We'll…'

The words faded into oblivion as some subtle change in his expression told her that that was not what this was about. He wasn't angry that she hadn't told Sarah they had to leave Thorn Trees. There was something else.

'Nikos…'

'Tell me about your mother.'

It was the last thing she had expected, and she knew that her consternation must show on her face as she stared at him.

'Tell me about your mother,' Nikos repeated. 'It seems to me that your problems with her are at the bottom of this situation. I know the signs.'

'What signs?'

'Tell me about your mother.'

He was clearly not going to concede an inch on this. And what could it hurt to tell him now? He had said the feud was over. She prayed that, for her mother's sake, he had meant it.

'She's ill,' Nikos said now.

'How did you…? Well, yes. She's—emotionally fragile. If you must know, she's agoraphobic—desperately so. She hasn't been out of the house in years. Not since George was born.'

She glanced nervously at Nikos, watching for his reaction. If he so much as looked shocked…

But Nikos simply nodded, his face calm, his expression attentive. With an elegant economy of movement he perched on the edge of the desk, one leg still resting on the floor, and waited.

'She—she had a breakdown after George was born—terrible postnatal depression combined with…with…'

'With the fact that her baby was not your father's,' Nikos put in, making Sadie blink in astonishment.

'How did you know?'

'It's the only thing that makes sense—all the secrecy about the child, the way your father behaved. Like a man betrayed. A man out to make the world pay for what had happened to him.'

'That was just how it was.' Sadie nodded sadly, remembering the dreadful fights, the constant yelling and screaming.

'Why didn't your mother leave him? Had her lover abandoned her?'

'He was dead. He died in an accident just before Mum found that she was pregnant. That was when my father found out too—and, well, everything together was just too much.'

'Did you ever find out who she had been seeing?'

'No. She would never say. And my father had made her promise that she never would. That was his condition for letting her stay. For not divorcing her. The only thing she ever told me was that he—her lover—drowned in a boating accident.'

'Over five years ago?'

What had she said to sharpen his tone, narrow his eyes like that?

'Is that important?'

But Nikos didn't answer her. Instead he was on his feet, pulling open a drawer in the desk.

'Do you have a photo of your brother?'

'Of George? Of course…' Rooting in her bag, she pulled out her wallet, opened it to where the passport-size picture was kept. 'But why?'

She took out the picture in the same moment that Nikos placed a large album on the desk, flicking through it until he found the photograph he wanted, one long bronzed finger pointing it out to her.

'Oh, my…'

Sadie let the picture she was holding drop down beside the one Nikos was indicating.

'It's George.'

'It's my Uncle Georgiou,' Nikos said flatly. 'When you were in here yesterday you commented on it specially, and since then it has been nagging at me. It was just before Georgiou died that your father really started to stick the knife into my father's company—it was one of the reasons why he was able to succeed so well so fast. Because when Dad was in mourning he was badly off balance—not focussing on business.'

'And my dad was hell-bent on revenge for Georgiou's affair with his wife!'

So much made sense now, in a way that it never had before.

'It wasn't just the feud—or rather it was that plus this new reason for anger, for revenge.'

And they had got caught up in it.

'That damn feud tainted every person it touched.'

Nikos's voice was filled with black anger and a touch of something else—something that Sadie would almost have labelled despair as he shook his dark head in disbelief over what had happened.

'But it really does end here.'

Suddenly he looked up, amber gaze burning straight into hers.

'It stops,' he said fiercely. 'And from now on things will be different. For a start, you will have no need to worry about Thorn Trees. The house will be my gift to your mother—and my cousin. And there will be more. Little George should have inherited all that his father had, and if he really is my uncle's son—and looking at this photo, I am sure that he is—then I will make sure he has what is his by right.'

'Thank you.'

Sadie made herself say it, though her tongue tripped up over the words. She found that her mind was seesawing from one emotion to another. She was full of relief for her mother, delight for George—but there was a terrible sense of uncertainty about what this would mean for herself. She had had to acknowledge that she had lost her chance of ever having Nikos love her. She had faced up to the prospect of a future without him and she had been prepared to leave. To head out into that future and try to cope with it as best she could. Now she saw that everything was going to be so much different. That with Nikos being George's cousin—George's family—inevitably he would want to be in the little boy's life. It was only right, only fair.

But it meant that she would frequently be forced to see this man she loved and who had never loved her. And she didn't know how she could handle that.

'It—it will mean a lot to my mother. She admitted to me recently that she adored George's father. That he was the love of her life. She was devastated when she learned he'd died.'

Suddenly something Nikos had said to start off this line of conversation came back to her, making her frown in confusion.

'When you asked about my mother—you said you knew the signs.'

The question she needed wouldn't form properly, but the urgency in her voice obviously hit home to Nikos and he nodded his understanding without her having to say any more.

'My father. I know what it's like to have to watch someone break down—to always feel that you need to check if they are all right. To worry that perhaps the depression will come back.'

'And this all stems from the same vile mess.'

She didn't have to ask, just as Nikos hadn't needed to ask her. His clouded eyes gave her the answer without words.

'When he lost everything—when your father took over everything and bankrupted him—it was soon after he'd lost his brother. Like your mother, he broke down. I came home one evening and found him...'

The way his face had lost colour warned that there had been something very wrong. Suddenly Nikos pushed himself from his seat on the desk and paced restively about the room, his actions like those of a wild hunting cat, caged up for far too long.

'I was early. I wasn't supposed to be there. He thought he had time.'

Suddenly Sadie thought she knew exactly what day Nikos had been talking about, and all the tiny hairs on the back of her neck lifted in fearful apprehension as Nikos paused in his restless pacing, standing by the window and staring out at the sea. But she was sure that those beautiful golden eyes saw nothing of the clear blue waves with their foamy white tops, the golden sands of the beach.

Nikos pressed his forehead against the window glass, closing his eyes in despair at his memories, and, seeing that, Sadie could not stay still at the other side of the room. In a rush she crossed to his side, reached out a hand and touched his arm, just above the elbow. It was all she dared do, even though her heart ached with misery at the way things had turned out.

Like their parents, both of them had been wounded, scarred by the dreadful feud between their families. But as a result of the fallout of that feud, a fallout that had tangled up their own lives, creating the mess they now lived with, neither of them could comfort the other properly.

'That was the day I rang you...'

The day when she had had second thoughts about her

father's warnings that Nikos was simply out to use her, to make her part of his revenge on the Carteret family because of the feud. She hadn't known then of his personal motives for making everything worse. She had broken off her engagement, cancelled her wedding at a day's notice, but she had wanted to at least try to talk to Nikos himself....

'You told me to go to hell.'

'I know.'

Nikos's sigh was weary, dragged up from somewhere deep inside him, and as he turned to her, his movements were slow and heavy, like those of a much older man.

'But what the hell else could I have done? I was there in a room with my father who thought he had lost everything. He'd got a gun from somewhere and he meant to use it on himself.'

'Oh, Nikos, no!'

It was worse than she had thought. Worse for Nikos and worse for herself.

Because of that phone call, and the way he had turned on her, she had moved herself firmly onto her father's side.

'I didn't know—and I believed that my dad was right. I begged him to help me, asked him to tell me how to handle things. He said that if I did as he told me, said exactly what he wanted me to say, then all would be well. He would even look after my mother, let her stay in the house. He would raise her baby as his own.'

And her father had given her the final, cruel words that she had tossed down the stairs to where Nikos was standing in the hall on that final day.

'I'm so sorry—I don't know how I could have said those dreadful things.'

'I do,' Nikos astounded her by replying. 'I know because I ended up getting caught in the same terrible mess. I was supposed to be helping my father, but I ended up getting so obsessed with you that I couldn't think straight. I took my eye off the ball—focussed on you, not the business. And then when I found that while you and I were in that cottage, away for the weekend…'

The look in his eyes told her without doubt exactly which weekend. The one she had arranged. The one where, half crazy with her physical hunger for this man, she had pushed him into anticipating his marriage vows. The resulting explosion of passion had kept them both locked in sensual obsession, barely even surfacing for food for the three days they were there.

For the space of the three days in which her father had finally made his move.

'I should have been there, checking on things, making sure he made no mistakes. Instead, I was the one who made the worst mistake.'

The 'worst mistake' being spending time with her. Sadie flinched inside at the pain of his words.

'I felt so terribly guilty as a result. I *was* guilty, and that guilt twisted me up inside. I blamed your family for everything that had happened—I blamed you.'

Pushing his fingers through his hair, Nikos pressed the heels of his hands against his temples, as if to ease some intolerable ache.

'So when you came to me for help—because your mother needed a home where she could be safe—I just saw the opportunity to take my revenge. *Thee mou,* my darling, I thought that I was immune to this damn feud and I was so proud of being so. Now I see that I was eaten up with it all the time. I thought the worst of you because that was what I expected from a member of the Carteret family. But I wasn't dealing with just one of the Carterets—I was dealing with you.'

Did he know what he had said? Sadie wondered, not daring

to ask the question for fear that, with the raw pain thickening Nikos's accent, she had misheard him and that 'my darling' had been something else entirely.

'You—you weren't completely to blame,' she stammered, feeling as if she was treading over delicate eggshells with infinite care. 'I had said some terrible things—done some…'

But Nikos was shaking his head again, his eyes dark and shadowed in a way that made her heart twist in pain.

'And even then I was deceiving myself. Even then I wasn't admitting to my real motives. I wasn't even acknowledging that revenge had nothing to do with it, not deep down. Deep down, from the moment I saw you again, I knew that I couldn't live without you in my life. That once I had you again I could never let you go. So I resorted to stupid subterfuge to get you here and keep you. I was sure that if we could just spend time together then it would be as it had always been.'

'It could—it was!' Sadie couldn't bear to let him go on berating himself any more. 'Didn't yesterday—last night—tell you something? That I wanted to be with you.'

'In my bed, perhaps,' Nikos responded heavily. 'But I wanted more than that. I wanted you in my life for good. And I was so desperate to do that that—to keep you with me—that I offered you anything—everything that I thought might keep you there. But I offered all the wrong things. You didn't want the house—or money…'

'No,' Sadie put in softly, her voice breaking suddenly as he reached out and took each of her hands in his, pulling her gently towards him. Her heart was racing so hard that it set her blood pounding in her ears, the sound like thunder inside her head. 'No, I don't want those.'

The hands that held hers tightened, drawing her even closer, so that they were almost touching, only their clasped hands coming between them, holding them just a breath apart.

The eyes that looked down into hers were blazingly intent, blindingly so. But now they were wide and clear, the clouds and the darkness burned away by the open sincerity that told her everything she needed to know.

'So now I'm going to offer you the only thing that really matters,' Nikos told her, his voice so deep, so serious, that it took her breath away, made her freeze into immobility, unable to blink or look away. 'Though the truth is that the only thing I have to give you, you already have. I gave it to you in the moment we met, but I never really knew it until now. As a result I've been lost and wandering—not knowing who to be or how to live.'

Suddenly, unexpectedly, he lowered himself slowly to the floor until he was on one knee at her feet, looking up into her face with his feelings clear and open for her to read.

'You have my heart, Sadie,' Nikos told her. 'You have my heart and my love—they are yours for ever, no matter what answer you give. I am yours. There is no other woman in the world for me. What I'm asking is will you be mine? Will you be my wife and help me to put this dreadful feud far behind us, to heal the hurts that it brought and create a future that is so different, so loving, that there will be nothing but bright days ahead of us?'

'Oh, Nikos…'

Sadie turned her hands in his so that she could hold him, draw him up again to face her, until she could look deep into his eyes and see the way they changed as she gave him her answer.

'You have my heart too, and I never, ever want it back. All I want is a chance to go into that future with you, to create those bright days and to love you as I have always wanted to do. And so of course my answer is yes. It never could be anything else. It's—'

But she never managed to get any more words out. Whatever she had been about to say was crushed into silence by the force and passion of the kiss that Nikos pressed against her lips. And as he swept her up into his arms, crushed her against him, she knew that no words were needed anyway.

Words were totally redundant when there were much better ways to express the way they were feeling.

'Can we go yet? Can we go?'

Little George was almost dancing on the spot in impatience, tapping his smart patent shoes on the floor and risking crumpling his crisp white shirt and pressed black trousers as he chanted his request over and over again.

'Can we go, pleeeease? I want to see Niko.'

'So do I,' Sadie told him, her smile mirroring that on her brother's face at the thought of the way that Nikos would be waiting for them, just a very short distance away on this special morning. 'And we'll be leaving very soon.'

George had adored his big cousin on sight, and in the time since they had first met that love had grown into a sort of idolatry as Nikos filled the role of the father the little boy had never had.

'But we just have to wait for—'

She broke off as the door opened and her mother, elegant in peach and cream, stepped into the room. Her eyes went straight to her daughter, taking in the full effect of the simple white sheath dress with its overskirt of lace, the simple wreath of flowers on Sadie's shining dark hair.

'You look gorgeous, my darling—every inch the beautiful bride. Nikos is going to be knocked for six when he sees you.'

'I hope so…' Sadie smoothed a hand down her dress as she drew in a deep calming breath. 'And what about you— are you OK, Mum?'

It was impossible to iron out the edge of concern in her voice as she studied her mother's face. Sarah looked calm and in control, but underneath her carefully applied make-up she was still slightly pale and drawn, revealing the effort she had made to be here. The therapist Nikos had found for her had worked wonders, and that, together with the new-found happiness that came from knowing all their worries about Thorn Trees and everything else were far behind them, had created an incredible transformation in her mother's life. But all the same the journey to Greece, to Icaros, was more than she had ever been able to imagine her mother could manage.

'I'm fine,' Sarah assured her now. 'I'm exactly where I want to be—by my daughter's side on her wedding day.'

'And I'm so happy that you're here with me.'

Happier than she could possibly put into words, Sadie told herself as she collected her bouquet of creamy roses. Today was literally the happiest day of her life. The day on which she was marrying the man she adored, and the day that marked once and for all the final ending of any last trace of the feud that had threatened to tear her and Nikos and their families apart.

Not only had she been welcomed into the Konstantos family, but George too had brought a new happiness to Nikos's father, the little boy's uncle. Petros had been overjoyed to find such a special link to his beloved dead brother in the little boy, and Sarah, as George's mother and the woman Georgiou had loved, had been gathered into the warmth and welcomed too.

'Can we go now?' George was chanting again. 'Is it time? I don't want to wait another minute.'

'It's time,' Sadie told him, keeping her bouquet in one hand as she held the other out to her mother. 'And I don't want to wait another minute, either.'

Arm in arm, with the little boy dancing around them, she and Sarah made their way out into the sunshine, taking the short walk towards the ancient wooden bridge, now beautifully decorated with flowers and ribbons that fluttered in the gentle breeze, leading to the open door of the tiny private chapel where Nikos waited for her.

Just for a moment, as she paused on the worn stone steps that led into the church, Sadie had a momentary flashback to the first time she had set foot inside the chapel. But that only lingered long enough for her to be able to drive it right out of her mind, knowing that such moments of doubt and insecurity were so far behind her now it was almost as if they had never happened. The promise of the happiness of her new life was now stretching out in front of her.

It took a moment for her eyes to adjust to the darkness inside the old building, but as soon as they did her gaze went straight to the tall, dark and powerful figure of the man standing at the altar.

Standing at the altar, waiting to make her his wife.

Immediately it was as if there was no one else in the place. As if the world and everyone in it had faded away and there was only this one man. The man to whom she had given her heart so completely that it was no longer a part of her but his to keep, to hold with him for ever.

'Nikos,' she breathed, tears of pure joy blurring his beloved image just for a moment.

It was impossible for him to have heard the sound of his name on her lips, but all the same in that instant something made Nikos turn and glance towards the back of the chapel. And the transformation that came over his face when he saw her standing there made her heart soar, her feet feel as if they were not touching the floor but floating inches above the worn stone flags.

'Sadie…'

She saw his lips move on her name, saw the smile that made his stunning eyes burn like bronze fire.

'Sadie—*kardia mou*—my love, my heart…'

When he held out both his hands to her, opening his arms wide to welcome her home, she didn't hesitate but practically flew the short distance down the aisle towards her future with the man she loved.

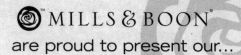

millsandboon.co.uk Community

Join Us!

The Community is the perfect place to meet and chat to kindred spirits who love books and reading as much as you do, but it's also the place to:

- **Get the inside scoop from authors about their latest books**
- **Learn how to write a romance book with advice from our editors**
- **Help us to continue publishing the best in women's fiction**
- **Share your thoughts on the books we publish**
- **Befriend other users**

Forums: Interact with each other as well as authors, editors and a whole host of other users worldwide.

Blogs: Every registered community member has their own blog to tell the world what they're up to and what's on their mind.

Book Challenge: We're aiming to read 5,000 books and have joined forces with The Reading Agency in our inaugural Book Challenge.

Profile Page: Showcase yourself and keep a record of your recent community activity.

Social Networking: We've added buttons at the end of every post to share via digg, Facebook, Google, Yahoo, technorati and de.licio.us.

www.millsandboon.co.uk

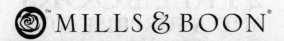

2 FREE BOOKS
AND A SURPRISE GIFT

We would like to take this opportunity to thank you for reading this Mills & Boon® book by offering you the chance to take TWO more specially selected books from the Modern™ series absolutely FREE! We're also making this offer to introduce you to the benefits of the Mills & Boon® Book Club™—

- **FREE home delivery**
- **FREE gifts and competitions**
- **FREE monthly Newsletter**
- **Exclusive Mills & Boon Book Club offers**
- **Books available before they're in the shops**

Accepting these FREE books and gift places you under no obligation to buy, you may cancel at any time, even after receiving your free books. Simply complete your details below and return the entire page to the address below. You don't even need a stamp!

YES Please send me 2 free Modern books and a surprise gift. I understand that unless you hear from me, I will receive 4 superb new books every month for just £3.19 each, postage and packing free. I am under no obligation to purchase any books and may cancel my subscription at any time. The free books and gift will be mine to keep in any case.

Ms/Mrs/Miss/Mr_____ Initials _____

Surname _____
Address _____
_____
_____ Postcode _____

Send this whole page to: Mills & Boon Book Club, Free Book Offer, FREEPOST NAT 10298, Richmond, TW9 1BR